John Ric

Wacousta; a tale of the Pontiac conspiracy; Volume Three of

in large print

John Richardson

Wacousta; a tale of the Pontiac conspiracy; Volume Three of

in large print

Reproduction of the original.

1st Edition 2023 | ISBN: 978-3-36833-624-0

Verlag (Publisher): Outlook Verlag GmbH, Zeilweg 44, 60439 Frankfurt, Deutschland
Vertretungsberechtigt (Authorized to represent): E. Roepke, Zeilweg 44, 60439 Frankfurt, Deutschland
Druck (Print): Books on Demand GmbH, In de Tarpen 42, 22848 Norderstedt, Deutschland

WACOUSTA;
OR
THE PROPHECY
a tale of the Pontiac conspiracy

By
John Richardson
Volume Three of Three

CHAPTER I.

The night passed away without further event on board the schooner, yet in all the anxiety that might be supposed incident to men so perilously situated. Habits of long-since acquired superstition, too powerful to be easily shaken off, moreover contributed to the dejection of the mariners, among whom there were not wanting those who believed the silent steersman was in reality what their comrade had represented,—an immaterial being, sent from the world of spirits to warn them of some impending evil. What principally gave weight to this impression were the repeated asseverations of Fuller, during the sleepless night passed by all on deck, that what he had seen was no other, could be no other, than a ghost! exhibiting in its hueless, fleshless cheek, the well-known lineaments of one who was supposed to be no more: and, if the story of their comrade had needed confirmation among men in whom faith in, rather than love for, the marvellous was a constitutional ingredient, the terrible effect that seemed to have been produced on Captain de Haldimar by the same mysterious visitation would have been more than conclusive. The very appearance of the night, too, favoured the delusion. The heavens, comparatively clear at the moment when the canoe approached the vessel, became suddenly enveloped in the deepest gloom at its departure, as if to enshroud the course of those who, having so mysteriously approached, had also so unaccountably disappeared. Nor had this threatening state of the atmosphere the counterbalancing advantage of storm and tempest to drive them onward through the narrow waters of the Sinclair, and enable them, by anticipating the pursuit of their enemies, to shun the Scylla and Charybdis that awaited their more leisure advance. The wind increased not; and the disappointed seamen remarked, with dismay, that their craft scarcely made more progress than at the moment when she first quitted her anchorage.

It was now near the first hours of day; and although, perhaps, none slept, there were few who were not apparently at rest, and plunged in the most painful reflections. Still occupying her humble couch, and shielded from the night air merely by the cloak that covered her own blood-stained garments, lay the unhappy Clara, her deep groans and stifled sobs bursting occasionally from her pent-up heart, and falling on the ears of the mariners like sounds of fearful import, produced by the mysterious agency that already bore such undivided power over their thoughts. On the bare deck, at her side, lay her brother, his face turned upon the planks, as if to shut out all objects from eyes he had not the power to close; and, with one arm supporting his heavy brow, while the other, cast around the restless form of his beloved sister, seemed to offer protection and to impart confidence, even while his lips denied the accents of consolation. Seated on an empty hen-coop at their head, was Sir Everard Valletort, his back reposing against the bulwarks of the vessel, his arms folded across his chest, and his eyes bent mechanically on the man at the helm, who stood within a few paces of him,—an attitude of absorption, which he, ever and anon, changed to one of anxious and enquiring interest, whenever the agitation of Clara was manifested in the manner already shown.

The main deck and forecastle of the vessel presented a similar picture of mingled unquietness and repose. Many of the seamen might be seen seated on the gun-carriages, with their cheeks pressing the rude metal that served them for a pillow. Others lay along the decks, with their heads resting on the elevated hatches; while not a few, squatted on their haunches with their knees doubled up to their very chins, supported in that position the aching head that rested between their rough and horny palms. A first glance might have induced the belief that all were buried in the most profound slumber; but the quick jerking of a limb,—the fitful, sudden shifting of a position,—the utter absence of that deep breathing which indicates the unconsciousness of repose, and the occasional spirting of tobacco juice upon the deck,—all these symptoms only required to be noticed, to prove the living silence that reigned throughout was not born either of apathy or sleep.

At the gangway at which the canoe had approached now stood the individual already introduced to our readers as Jack Fuller. The same superstitious terror that caused his flight had once more attracted him to the spot where the subject of his alarm first appeared to him; and, without seeming to reflect that the vessel, in her slow but certain progress, had left all vestige of the mysterious visitant behind, he continued gazing over the bulwarks on the dark waters, as if he expected at each moment to find his sight stricken by the same appalling vision. It was at the moment when he had worked up his naturally dull imagination to its highest perception of the supernatural, that he was joined by the rugged boatswain, who had passed the greater part of the night in pacing up and down the decks, watching the aspect of the heavens, and occasionally tauting a rope or squaring a light yard, unassisted, as the fluttering of the canvass in the wind rendered the alteration necessary.

"Well, Jack!" bluntly observed the latter in a gruff whisper that resembled the suppressed growling of a mastiff, "what the hell are ye thinking of now?—Not got over your flumbustification yet, that ye stand here, looking as sanctified as an old parson!"

"I'll tell ye what it is, Mr. Mullins," returned the sailor, in the same key; "you may make as much game on me as you like; but these here strange sort of doings are somehow quizzical; and, though I fears nothing in the shape of flesh and blood, still, when it comes to having to do with those as is gone to Davy Jones's locker like, it gives a fellow an all-overishness as isn't quite the thing. You understand me?"

"I'm damned if I do!" was the brief but energetic rejoinder.

"Well, then," continued Fuller, "if I must out with it, I must. I think that 'ere Ingian must have been the devil, or how could he come so sudden and unbeknownst upon me, with the head of a 'possum: and then, agin, how could he get away from the craft without our seeing him? and how came the ghost on board of the canoe?"

"Avast there, old fellow; you means not the head of a 'possum, but a beaver: but that 'ere's all nat'r'l enough, and easily 'counted for; but you hav'n't told us whose ghost it was, after all."

"No; the captain made such a spring to the gunwale, as frighted it all out of my head: but come closer, Mr. Mullins, and I'll whisper it in your ear.—Hark! what was that?"

"I hears nothing," said the boatswain, after a pause.

"It's very odd," continued Fuller; "but I thought as how I heard it several times afore you came."

"There's something wrong, I take it, in your upper story, Jack Fuller," coolly observed his companion; "that 'ere ghost has quite capsized you."

"Hark, again!" repeated the sailor. "Didn't you hear it then? A sort of a groan like."

"Where, in what part?" calmly demanded the boatswain, though in the same suppressed tone in which the dialogue had been, carried on.

"Why, from the canoe that lies alongside there. I heard it several times afore."

"Well, damn my eyes, if you a'rn't turned a real coward at last," politely remarked Mr. Mullins. "Can't the poor fat devil of a Canadian snooze a bit in his hammock, without putting you so completely out of your reckoning?"

"The Canadian—the Canadian!" hurriedly returned Fuller: "why, don't you see him there, leaning with his back to the main-mast, and as fast asleep as if the devil himself couldn't wake him?"

"Then it was the devil, you heard, if you like," quaintly retorted Mullins: "but bear a hand, and tell us all about this here ghost."

"Hark, again! what was that?" once more enquired the excited sailor.

"Only a gust of wind passing through the dried boughs of the canoe," said the boatswain: "but since we can get nothing out of that crazed noddle of yours, see if you can't do

8

something with your hands. That 'ere canoe running alongside, takes half a knot off the ship's way. Bear a hand then, and cast off the painter, and let her drop astarn, that she may follow in our wake. Hilloa! what the hell's the matter with the man now?"

And well might he ask. With his eyeballs staring, his teeth chattering, his body half bent, and his arms thrown forward, yet pendent as if suddenly arrested in that position while in the act of reaching the rope, the terrified sailor stood gazing on the stern of the canoe; in which, by the faint light of the dawning day, was to be seen an object well calculated to fill the least superstitious heart with terror and dismay. Through an opening in the foliage peered the pale and spectral face of a human being, with its dull eyes bent fixedly and mechanically upon the vessel. In the centre of the wan forehead was a dark incrustation, as of blood covering the superficies of a newly closed wound. The pallid mouth was partially unclosed, so as to display a row of white and apparently lipless teeth; and the features were otherwise set and drawn, as those of one who is no longer of earth. Around the head was bound a covering so close, as to conceal every part save the face; and once or twice a hand was slowly raised, and pressed upon the blood spot that dimmed the passing fairness of the brow. Every other portion of the form was invisible.

"Lord have mercy upon us!" exclaimed the boatswain, in a voice that, now elevated to more than its natural tone, sounded startlingly on the stillness of the scene; "sure enough it is, indeed, a ghost!"

"Ha! do you believe me now?" returned Fuller, gaining confidence from the admission of his companion, and in the same elevated key. "It is, as I hope to be saved, the ghost I see'd afore."

The commotion on deck was now every where universal. The sailors started to their feet, and, with horror and alarm visibly imprinted on their countenances, rushed tumultuously towards the dreaded gangway.

"Make way—room, fellows!" exclaimed a hurried voice; and presently Captain de Haldimar, who had bounded like lightning from the deck, appeared with eager eye and excited cheek among them. To leap into the bows of the canoe, and disappear under the foliage, was the work of a single instant. All listened breathlessly for the slightest sound; and then every heart throbbed with the most undefinable emotions, as his lips were heard giving utterance to the deep emotion of his own spirit,—

"Madeline, oh, my own lost Madeline!" he exclaimed with almost frantic energy of passion: "do I then press you once more in madness to my doting heart? Speak, speak to me—

10

for God's sake speak, or I shall go mad! Air, air,—she wants air only—she cannot be dead."

These last words were succeeded by the furious rending asunder of the fastenings that secured the boughs, and presently the whole went overboard, leaving revealed the tall and picturesque figure of the officer; whose left arm encircled while it supported the reclining and powerless form of one who well resembled, indeed, the spectre for which she had been mistaken, while his right hand was busied in detaching the string that secured a portion of the covering round her throat. At length it fell from her shoulders; and the well known form of Madeline de Haldimar, clad even in the vestments in which they had been wont to see her, met the astonished gaze of the excited seamen. Still there were some who doubted it was the corporeal woman whom they beheld; and several of the crew who were catholics even made the sign of the cross as the supposed spirit was now borne up the gangway in the arms of the pained yet gratified De Haldimar: nor was it until her feet were seen finally resting on the deck, that Jack Fuller could persuade himself it was indeed Miss de Haldimar, and not her ghost, that lay clasped to the heart of the officer.

With the keen rush of the morning air upon her brow returned the suspended consciousness of the bewildered Madeline. The blood came slowly and imperceptibly to her cheek; and her eyes, hitherto glazed, fixed, and inexpressive,

11

looked enquiringly, yet with stupid wonderment, around. She started from the embrace of her lover, gazed alternately at his disguise, at himself, and at Clara; and then passing her hand several times rapidly across her brow, uttered an hysteric scream, and threw herself impetuously forward on the bosom of the sobbing girl; who, with extended arms, parted lips, and heaving bosom, sat breathlessly awaiting the first dawn of the returning reason of her more than sister.

We should vainly attempt to paint all the heart-rending misery of the scene exhibited in the gradual restoration of Miss de Haldimar to her senses. From a state of torpor, produced by the freezing of every faculty into almost idiocy, she was suddenly awakened to all the terrors of the past and the deep intonations of her rich voice were heard only in expressions of agony, that entered into the most iron-hearted of the assembled seamen; while they drew from the bosom of her gentle and sympathising cousin fresh bursts of desolating grief. Imagination itself would find difficulty in supplying the harrowing effect upon all, when, with upraised hands, and on her bended knees, her large eyes turned wildly up to heaven, she invoked in deep and startling accents the terrible retribution of a just God on the inhuman murderers of her father, with whose life-blood her garments were profusely saturated; and then, with hysteric laughter, demanded why she alone had been singled out to survive the bloody tragedy. Love and affection, hitherto the first principles of her existence, then found no entrance into her mind. Stricken, broken-hearted, stultified to all feeling save that of her immediate wretchedness, she thought only of the horrible scenes through which she had passed; and even he, whom at another moment she could have clasped in an agony of fond tenderness to her beating bosom,—he to whom she had pledged her virgin faith, and was bound by the dearest of human ties,—he whom she had so often longed to behold once more, and had thought of, the preceding day, with all the tenderness of her impassioned and devoted soul,—even he did not, in the first hours of her terrible consciousness, so much as command a single passing regard. All the affections were for a period blighted in her bosom. She seemed as one devoted, without the power of resistance, to a grief which calcined and preyed upon all other feelings of the mind. One stunning and annihilating reflection seemed to engross every principle of her being; nor was it for hours after she had been restored to life and recollection that a deluge of burning tears, giving relief to her heart and a new direction to her feelings, enabled her at length to separate the past from, and in some degree devote herself to, the present. Then, indeed, for the first time did she perceive and take pleasure in the presence of her lover; and clasping her beloved and weeping Clara to her heart, thank her God, in all the fervour of true piety, that she at least had been spared to shed a ray of comfort on her distracted spirit. But we will not pain the reader by dwelling

13

on a scene that drew tears even from the rugged and flint-nerved boatswain himself; for, although we should linger on it with minute anatomical detail, no powers of language we possess could convey the transcript as it should be. Pass we on, therefore, to the more immediate incidents of our narrative.

The day now rapidly developing, full opportunity was afforded the mariners to survey the strict nature of their position. To all appearance they were yet in the middle of the lake, for around them lay the belting sweep of forest that bounded the perspective of the equidistant circle, of which their bark was the focus or immediate centre. The wind was dying gradually away, and when at length the sun rose, in all his splendour, there was scarce air enough in the heavens to keep the sails from flapping against the masts, or to enable the vessel to obey her helm. In vain was the low and peculiar whistle of the seamen heard, ever and anon, in invocation of the departing breeze. Another day, calm and breathless as the preceding, had been chartered from the world of light; and their hearts failed them, as they foresaw the difficulty of their position, and the almost certainty of their retreat being cut off. It was while labouring under the disheartening consciousness of danger, peculiar to all, that the anxious boatswain summoned Captain de Haldimar and Sir Everard Valletort, by a significant beck of the finger, to the side of the deck opposite to that on which still lay the suffering and nearly broken-hearted girls.

"Well, Mullins, what now?" enquired the former, as he narrowly scanned the expression of the old man's features: "that clouded brow of yours, I fear me, bodes no agreeable information."

"Why, your honour, I scarcely knows what to say about it; but seeing as I'm the only officer in the ship, now our poor captain is killed, God bless him! I thought I might take the liberty to consult with your honours as to the best way of getting out of the jaws of them sharks of Ingians; and two heads, as the saying is, is always better than one."

"And now you have the advantage of three," observed the officer, with a sickly smile; "but I fear, Mullins, that if your own be not sufficient for the purpose, ours will be of little service. You must take counsel from your own experience and knowledge of nautical matters."

"Why, to be sure, your honour," and the sailor rolled his quid from one cheek to the other, "I think I may say as how I'll venture to steer the craft with any man on the Canada lakes, and bring her safe into port too; but seeing as how I'm only a petty officer, and not yet recommended by his worship the governor for the full command, I thought it but right to consult with my superiors, not as to the management of the craft, but the best as is to be done. What

15

does your honour think of making for the high land over the larboard bow yonder, and waiting for the chance of the night-breeze to take us through the Sinclair?"

"Do whatever you think best," returned the officer. "For my part, I scarcely can give an opinion. Yet how are we to get there? There does not appear to be a breath of wind."

"Oh, that's easily managed; we have only to brail and furl up a little, to hide our cloth from the Ingians, and then send the boats a-head to tow the craft, while some of us lend a hand at her own sweeps. We shall get close under the lee of the land afore night, and then we must pull up agin along shore, until we get within a mile or so of the head of the river."

"But shall we not be seen by our enemies?" asked Sir Everard; "and will they not be on the watch for our movements, and intercept our retreat?"

"Now that's just the thing, your honour, as they're not likely to do, if so be as we bears away for yon headlands. I knows every nook and sounding round the lake; and odd enough if I didn't, seeing as how the craft circumnavigated it, at least, a dozen times since we have been cooped up here. Poor Captain Danvers! (may the devil damn his murderers, I say, though it does make a commander of me for once;) he used always to make for that 'ere point, whenever he wished to lie quiet; for never once did we see so much as a single

Ingian on the headland. No, your honour, they keeps all at t'other side of the lake, seeing as how that is the main road from Mackina' to Detroit."

"Then, by all means, do so," eagerly returned Captain de Haldimar. "Oh, Mullins! take us but safely through, and if the interest of my father can procure you a king's commission, you shall not want it, believe me."

"And if half my fortune can give additional stimulus to exertion, it shall be shared, with pleasure, between yourself and crew," observed Sir Everard.

"Thank your honours,—thank your honours," said the boatswain, somewhat electrified by these brilliant offers. "The lads may take the money, if they like; all I cares about is the king's commission. Give me but a swab on my shoulder, and the money will come fast enough of itself. But, still, shiver my topsails, if I wants any bribery to make me do my duty; besides, if 'twas only for them poor girls alone, I would go through fire and water to sarve them. I'm not very chicken-hearted in my old age, your honours, but I don't recollect the time when I blubbered so much as I did when Miss Madeline come aboard. But I can't bear to think of it; and now let us see and get all ready for towing."

Every thing now became bustle and activity on board the schooner. The matches, no longer required for the moment, were extinguished, and the heavy cutlasses and pistols unbuckled from the loins of the men, and deposited near their respective guns. Light forms flew aloft, and, standing out upon the yards, loosely furled the sails that had previously been hauled and clewed up; but, as this was an operation requiring little time in so small a vessel, those who were engaged in it speedily glided to the deck again, ready for a more arduous service. The boats had, meanwhile, been got forward, and into these the sailors sprang, with an alacrity that could scarcely have been expected from men who had passed not only the preceding night, but many before it, in utter sleeplessness and despair. But the imminence of the danger, and the evident necessity existing for exertion, aroused them to new energy; and the hitherto motionless vessel was now made to obey the impulse given by the tow ropes of the boats, in a manner that proved their crews to have entered on their toil with the determination of men, resolved to devote themselves in earnest to their task. Nor was the spirit of action confined to these. The long sweeps of the schooner had been shipped, and such of the crew as remained on board laboured effectually at them,—a service, in which they were essentially aided, not only by mine host of the Fleur de lis, but by the young officers themselves.

At mid-day the headlands were seen looming largely in the distance, while the immediate shores of the ill-fated fortress were momentarily, and in the same proportion, disappearing under the dim line of horizon in the rear. More than half their course, from the spot whence they commenced towing, had been completed, when the harassed men were made to quit their oars, in order to partake of the scanty fare of the vessel, consisting chiefly of dried bear's meat and venison. Spirit of any description they had none; but, unlike their brethren of the Atlantic, when driven to extremities in food, they knew not what it was to poison the nutritious properties of the latter by sipping the putrid dregs of the water-cask, in quantities scarce sufficient to quench the fire of their parched palates. Unslaked thirst was a misery unknown to the mariners of these lakes: it was but to cast their buckets deep into the tempting element, and water, pure, sweet, and grateful as any that ever bubbled from the moss-clad fountain of sylvan deity, came cool and refreshing to their lips, neutralising, in a measure, the crudities of the coarsest food. It was to this inestimable advantage the crew of the schooner had been principally indebted for their health, during the long series of privation, as far as related to fresh provisions and rest, to which they had been subjected. All appeared as vigorous in frame, and robust in health, as at the moment when they had last quitted the waters of the Detroit; and but for the inward sinking of the spirit, reflected in many a bronzed and furrowed brow, there was little to show they had been exposed to any very extraordinary trials.

Their meal having been hastily dispatched, and sweetened by a draught from the depths of the Huron, the seamen once more sprang into their boats, and devoted themselves, heart and soul, to the completion of their task, pulling with a vigour that operated on each and all with a tendency to encouragement and hope. At length the vessel, still impelled by her own sweeps, gradually approached the land; and at rather more than an hour before sunset was so near that the moment was deemed arrived when, without danger of being perceived, she might be run up along the shore to the point alluded to by the boatswain. Little more than another hour was occupied in bringing her to her station; and the red tints of departing day were still visible in the direction of the ill-fated fortress of Michilimackinac, when the sullen rumbling of the cable, following the heavy splash of the anchor, announced the place of momentary concealment had been gained.

The anchorage lay between two projecting headlands; to the outermost extremities of which were to be seen, overhanging the lake, the stately birch and pine, connected at their base by an impenetrable brushwood, extending to the very shore, and affording the amplest concealment, except from the lake side and the banks under which the schooner was moored. From the first quarter, however, little danger was incurred, as any canoes the savages might send in discovery of their course, must unavoidably be seen the moment they appeared over the line of the horizon, while, on the contrary, their own vessel, although much larger, resting on and identified with the land, must be invisible, except on a very near approach. In the opposite direction they were equally safe; for, as Mullins had truly remarked, none, save a few wandering hunters, whom chance occasionally led to the spot, were to be met with in a part of the country that lay so completely out of the track of communication between the fortresses. It was, however, but to double the second headland in their front, and they came within view of the Sinclair, the head of which was situated little more than a league beyond the spot where they now lay. Thus secure for the present, and waiting only for the rising of the breeze, of which the setting sun had given promise, the sailors once more snatched their hasty refreshment, while two of their number were sent aloft to keep a vigilant look-out along the circuit embraced by the enshrouding headlands.

During the whole of the day the cousins had continued on deck clasped in each other's arms, and shedding tears of bitterness, and heaving the most heart-rending sobs at intervals, yet but rarely conversing. The feelings of both were too much oppressed to admit of the utterance of their grief. The vampire of despair had banqueted on their hearts. Their vitality had been sucked, as it were, by its cold and bloodless lips; and little more than the withered rind, that had contained the seeds of so many affections, had been left.

21

Often had Sir Everard and De Haldimar paused momentarily from the labour of their oars, to cast an eye of anxious solicitude on the scarcely conscious girls, wishing, rather than expecting, to find the violence of their desolation abated, and that, in the full expansion of unreserved communication, they were relieving their sick hearts from the terrible and crushing weight of woe that bore them down. Captain de Haldimar had even once or twice essayed to introduce the subject himself, in the hope that some fresh paroxysm, following their disclosures, would remove the horrible stupefaction of their senses; but the wild look and excited manner of Madeline, whenever he touched on the chord of her affliction, had as often caused him to desist.

Towards the evening, however, her natural strength of character came in aid of his quiescent efforts to soothe her; and she appeared not only more composed, but more sensible of the impression produced by surrounding objects. As the last rays of the sun were tinging the horizon, she drew up her form in a sitting position against the bulwarks, and, raising her clasped hands to heaven, while her eyes were bent long and fixedly on the distant west, appeared for some minutes wholly lost in that attitude of absorption. Then she closed her eyes; and through the swollen lids came coursing, one by one, over her quivering cheek, large tears, that seemed to scald a furrow where they passed. After this she became more calm—her respiration more free; and she even consented to taste the humble meal which the young man now offered for the third time. Neither Clara nor herself had eaten food since the preceding morning; and the weakness of their frames contributed not a little to the increasing despondency of their spirits; but, notwithstanding several attempts previously made, they had rejected what was offered them, with insurmountable loathing. When they had now swallowed a few morsels of the sliced venison ham, prepared with all the delicacy the nearly exhausted resources of the vessel could supply, accompanied by a small portion of the cornbread of the Canadian, Captain de Haldimar prevailed on them to swallow a few drops of the spirit that still remained in the canteen given them by Erskine on their departure from Detroit. The genial liquid sent a kindling glow to their chilled hearts, and for a moment deadened the pungency of their anguish; and then it was that Miss de Haldimar entered briefly on the horrors she had witnessed, while Clara, with her arm encircling her waist, fixed her dim and swollen eyes, from which a tear ever and anon rolled heavily to her lap, on those of her beloved cousin.

CHAPTER II.

Without borrowing the affecting language of the unhappy girl—a language rendered even more touching by the peculiar pathos of her tones, and the searching agony of spirit that burst at intervals through her narrative—we will merely present our readers with a brief summary of what was gleaned from her melancholy disclosure. On bearing her cousin to the bedroom, after the terrifying yell first heard from without the fort, she had flown down the front stairs of the blockhouse, in the hope of reaching the guardroom in time to acquaint Captain Baynton with what she and Clara had witnessed from their window. Scarcely, however, had she gained the exterior of the building, when she saw that officer descending from a point of the rampart immediately on her left, and almost in a line with the block-house. He was running to overtake and return the ball of the Indian players, which had, at that moment, fallen into the centre of the fort, and was now rolling rapidly away from the spot on which Miss de Haldimar stood. The course of the ball led the pursuing officer out of the reach of her voice; and it was not until he had overtaken and thrown it again over the rampart, she could succeed in claiming his attention. No sooner, however, had he heard her hurried statement, than, without waiting to take the orders of his commanding officer, he prepared to join his guard, and give directions for the immediate closing of the gates. But the opportunity was now lost. The delay occasioned by the chase and recovery of the ball had given the Indians time to approach the gates in a body, while the unsuspicious soldiery looked on without so much as dreaming to prevent them; and Captain Baynton had scarcely moved forward in execution of his purpose, when the yelling fiends were seen already possessing themselves of the drawbridge, and exhibiting every appearance of fierce hostility. Wild, maddened at the sight, the almost frantic Madeline, alive only to her father's danger, rushed back towards the council-room, whence the startling yell from without had already been echoed, and where the tramp of feet, and the clashing of weapons, were distinguishable.

Cut off from his guard, by the rapid inundation of warriors, Captain Baynton had at once seen the futility of all attempts to join the men, and his first impression evidently had been to devote himself to the preservation of the cousins. With this view he turned hastily to Miss de Haldimar, and hurriedly naming the back staircase of the block-house, urged her to direct her flight to that quarter. But the excited girl had neither consideration nor fear for herself; she thought only of her father: and, even while the fierceness of contest was at its height within, she suddenly burst into the council-room. The confusion and horror of the scene that met her eyes no language can render: blood was flowing in every direction, and dying and dead officers, already stripped of their scalps, were lying strewed about the room. Still the survivors fought with all the obstinacy of despair, and many of the Indians had shared the fate of their victims. Miss de Haldimar attempted to reach her father, then vigorously combating with one of the most desperate of the chiefs; but, before she could dart through the intervening crowd, a savage seized her by the hair, and brandished a tomahawk rapidly over her neck. At that moment Captain Baynton sent his glittering blade deep into the heart of the Indian, who, relinquishing his grasp, fell dead at the feet of his intended victim. The devoted officer then threw his left arm round her waist, and, parrying with his sword-arm the blows of those who sought to intercept his flight, dragged his reluctant burden towards the door. Hotly pressed by the remaining officers, nearly equal in number, the Indians were now compelled to turn and defend themselves in front, when Captain Baynton took that opportunity of getting once more into the corridor, not, however, without having received a severe wound immediately behind the right ear, and leaving a skirt and lappel of his uniform in the hands of two savages who had successively essayed to detain him. At that moment the band without had succeeded in forcing open the door of the guard-room; and the officer saw, at a glance, there was little time left for decision. In hurried and imploring accents he besought Miss de Haldimar to forget every thing but her own danger, and to summon resolution to tear herself from the scene: but prayer and entreaty, and even force, were alike employed in vain. Clinging firmly to the rude balustrades, she refused to be led up the staircase, and wildly resisting all his efforts to detach her hands, declared she would again return to the scene of death, in which her beloved parent was so conspicuous an actor. While he was yet engaged in this fruitless attempt to force her from the spot, the door of the council-room was suddenly burst open, and a group of bleeding officers, among whom was Major de Haldimar, followed by their yelling enemies, rushed wildly into the passage, and, at the very foot of the stairs where they yet stood, the combat was renewed. From that moment Miss de Haldimar lost sight of her generous protector. Meanwhile the tumult of execrations, and groans, and yells, was at its height; and one by one she saw the unhappy officers sink beneath weapons yet reeking with the blood of their comrades, until not more than three or four, including her father and the commander of the schooner, were left. At length Major de Haldimar, overcome by exertion, and faint from wounds, while his wild eye darted despairingly on his daughter, had his sword-arm desperately wounded, when the blade dropped to the earth, and a dozen weapons glittered above his head. The wild shriek that had startled Clara then burst from the agonised heart of her maddened cousin, and she darted forward to cover her father's head with her arms. But her senses failed her in the attempt; and the last thing she recollected was falling over the weltering form of Middleton, who pressed her, as she lay there, in the convulsive energy of death, to his almost pulseless heart.

A vague consciousness of being raised from the earth, and borne rapidly through the air, came over her even in the midst of her insensibility, but without any definite perception of the present, or recollection of the past, until she suddenly, when about midway between the fort and the point of wood that led to Chabouiga, opened her eyes, and found herself in the firm grasp of an Indian, whose features, even in the hasty and fearful glance she cast at the countenance, she fancied were not unfamiliar to her. Not another human being was to be seen in the clearing at that moment; for all the savages, including even the women assembled outside, were now within the fort assisting in the complex horrors of murder, fire, and spoliation. In the wild energy of returning reason and despair, the wretched girl struggled violently to free herself; and so far with success, that the Indian, whose strength was evidently fast failing him, was compelled to quit his hold, and suffer her to walk. No sooner did Miss de Haldimar feel her feet touching the ground, when she again renewed her exertions to free herself, and return to the fort; but the Indian held her firmly secured by a leathern thong he now attached to her waist, and every attempt proved abortive. He was evidently much disconcerted at her resistance; and more than once she expected, and almost hoped, the tomahawk at his side would be made to revenge him for the test to which his patience was subjected; but Miss de Haldimar looked in vain for the expression of ferocity and impatience that might have been expected from him at such a moment. There was an air of mournfulness, and even kindness, mingled with severity, on his smooth brow that harmonised ill with the horrible atrocities in which he had, to all appearance, covered as he was with blood, been so recent and prominent an actor. The Indian remarked her surprise; and then looking hurriedly, yet keenly, around, and finding no living being near them, suddenly tore the shirt from his chest, and emphatically pronouncing the names "Oucanasta," "De Haldimar," disclosed to the still struggling captive the bosom of a woman. After which, pointing in the direction of the wood, and finally towards Detroit, she gave Miss de Haldimar to understand that was the course intended to be pursued.

In a moment the resistance of the latter ceased. She at once recognised the young Indian woman whom her cousin had rescued from death: and aware, as she was, of the strong attachment that had subsequently bound her to her preserver, she was at no loss to understand how she might have been led to devote herself to the rescue of one whom, it was probable, she knew to be his affianced wife. Once, indeed, a suspicion of a different nature crossed her mind; for the thought occurred to her she had only been saved from the general doom to be made the victim of private revenge—that it was only to glut the jealous vengeance of the woman at a more deliberative hour, she had been made a temporary captive. The apprehension, however, was no sooner formed than extinguished. Bitterly, deeply as she had reason to abhor the treachery and cunning of the dark race to which her captor belonged, there was an expression of openness and sincerity, and even imploringness, in the countenance of Oucanasta, which, added to her former knowledge of the woman, at once set this fear at rest, inducing her to look upon her rather in the character of a disinterested saviour, than in that of a cruel and vindictive enemy, goaded on to the indulgence of malignant hate by a spirit of rivalry and revenge. Besides, even were her cruellest fears to be realised, what could await her worse than the past? If she could even succeed in getting away, it would only be to return upon certain death; and death only could await her, however refined the tortures accompanying its infliction, in the event of her quietly following and yielding herself up to the guidance of one who offered this slight consolation, at least, that she was of her own sex. But Miss de Haldimar was willing to attribute more generous motives to the Indian; and fortified in her first impression, she signified by signs, that seemed to be perfectly intelligible to her companion, she appreciated her friendly intentions, and confided wholly in her.

No longer checked in her efforts, Oucanasta now directed her course towards the wood, still holding the thong that remained attached to Miss de Haldimar's waist, probably with a view to deceive any individuals from the villages on whom they might chance to fall, into a belief that the English girl was in reality her prisoner. No sooner, however, had they entered the depths of the forest, when, instead of following the path that led to Chabouiga, Oucanasta took a direction to the left, and then moving nearly on a parallel line with the course of the lake, continued her flight as rapidly as the rude nature of the underwood, and the unpractised feet of her companion, would permit. They had travelled in this manner for upwards of four hours, without meeting a breathing thing, or even so much as exchanging a sound between themselves, when, at length, the Indian stopped at the edge of a deep cavern-like excavation in the earth, produced by the tearing up, by the wild tempest, of an enormous pine. Into this she descended, and presently reappeared with several blankets, and two light painted paddles. Then unloosing the thong from the waist of the exhausted girl, she proceeded to disguise her in one of the blankets in the manner already shown, securing it over the head, throat, and shoulders with the badge of captivity, now no longer necessary for her purpose. She then struck off at right angles from the course they had previously pursued; and in less than twenty minutes both stood on the lake shore, apparently at a great distance from the point whence

31

they had originally set out. The Indian gazed for a moment anxiously before her; and then, with an exclamation, evidently meant to convey a sense of pleasure and satisfaction, pointed forward upon the lake. Miss de Haldimar followed, with eager and aching eyes, the direction of her finger, and beheld the well-known schooner evidently urging her flight towards the entrance of the Sinclair. Oh, how her sick heart seemed ready to burst at that moment! When she had last gazed upon it was from the window of her favourite apartment; and even while she held her beloved Clara clasped fondly in her almost maternal embrace, she had dared to indulge the fairest images that ever sprung into being at the creative call of woman's fancy. How bitter had been the reverse! and what incidents to fill up the sad volume of the longest life of sorrow and bereavement had not Heaven awarded her in lieu! In one short hour the weight of a thousand worlds had fallen on and crushed her heart; and when and how was the panacea to be obtained to restore one moment's cessation from suffering to her agonised spirit? Alas! she felt at that moment, that, although she should live a thousand years, the bitterness and desolation of her grief must remain. From the vessel she turned her eyes away upon the distant shore, which it was fast quitting, and beheld a column of mingled flame and smoke towering far above the horizon, and attesting the universal wreck of what had so long been endeared to her as her home. And she had witnessed all this, and yet had strength to survive it!

The courage of the unhappy girl had hitherto been sustained by no effort of volition of her own. From the moment when, discovering a friend in Oucanasta, she had yielded herself unresistingly to the guidance of that generous creature, her feelings had been characterised by an obtuseness strongly in contrast with the high excitement that had distinguished her previous manner. A dreamy recollection of some past horror, it is true, pursued her during her rapid and speechless flight; but any analysis of the causes conducing to that horror, her subjugated faculties were unable to enter upon. Even as one who, under the influence of incipient slumber, rejects the fantastic images that rise successively and indistinctly to the slothful brain, until, at length, they weaken, fade, and gradually die away, leaving nothing but a formless and confused picture of the whole; so was it with Miss de Haldimar. Had she been throughout alive to the keen recollections associated with her flight, she could not have stirred a foot in furtherance of her own safety, even if she would. The mere instinct of self-preservation would never have won one so truly devoted to the generous purpose of her deliverer, had not the temporary stupefaction of her mind prevented all desire of opposition. It is true, in the moment of her discovery of the sex of Oucanasta, she had been able to exercise her reflecting

33

powers; but they were only in connection with the present, and wholly abstract and separate from the past. She had followed her conductor almost without consciousness, and with such deep absorption of spirit, that she neither once conjectured whither they were going, nor what was to be the final issue of their flight. But now, when she stood on the lake shore, suddenly awakened, as if by some startling spell, to every harrowing recollection, and with her attention assisted by objects long endeared, and rendered familiar to her gaze—when she beheld the vessel that had last borne her across the still bosom of the Huron, fleeing for ever from the fortress where her arrival had been so joyously hailed—when she saw that fortress itself presenting the hideous spectacle of a blackened mass of ruins fast crumbling into nothingness—when, in short, she saw nothing but what reminded her of the terrific past, the madness of reason returned, and the desolation of her heart was complete. And then, again, when she thought of her generous, her brave, her beloved, and too unfortunate father, whom she had seen perish at her feet—when she thought of her own gentle Clara, and the sufferings and brutalities to which, if she yet lived, she must inevitably be exposed, and of the dreadful fate of the garrison altogether, the most menial of whom was familiar to her memory, brought up, as she had been, among them from her childhood—when she dwelt on all these things, a faintness, as of death, came over her, and she sank without life on the beach. Of what passed afterwards she had no recollection. She neither knew how she had got into the canoe, nor what means the Indian had taken to secure her approach to the schooner. She had no consciousness of having been removed to the bark of the Canadian, nor did she even remember having risen and gazed through the foliage on the vessel at her side; but she presumed, the chill air of morning having partially restored pulsation, she had moved instinctively from her recumbent position to the spot in which her spectre-like countenance had been perceived by Fuller. The first moment of her returning reason was that when, standing on the deck of the schooner, she found herself so unexpectedly clasped to the heart of her lover.

Twilight had entirely passed away when Miss de Haldimar completed her sad narrative; and already the crew, roused to exertion by the swelling breeze, were once more engaged in weighing the anchor, and setting and trimming the sails of the schooner, which latter soon began to shoot round the concealing headland into the opening of the Sinclair. A deathlike silence prevailed throughout the decks of the little bark, as her bows, dividing the waters of the basin that formed its source, gradually immerged into the current of that deep but narrow river; so narrow, indeed, that from its centre the least active of the mariners might have leaped without difficulty to either shore. This was the most critical part of the dangerous navigation. With a wide sea-board, and full command of their helm, they had nothing to fear; but so limited was the passage of this river, it was with difficulty the yards and masts of the schooner could be kept disengaged from the projecting boughs of the dense forest that lined the adjacent shores to their very junction with the water. The darkness of the night, moreover, while it promised to shield them from the observation of the savages, contributed greatly to perplex their movements; for such was the abruptness with which the river wound itself round in various directions, that it required a man constantly on the alert at the bows to apprise the helmsman of the course he should steer, to avoid collision with the shores. Canopies of weaving branches met in various directions far above their heads, and through these the schooner glided with a silence that might have called up the idea of a Stygian freight. Meanwhile, the men stood anxiously to their guns, concealing the matches in their water-buckets as before; and, while they strained both ear and eye through the surrounding; gloom to discover the slightest evidence of danger, grasped the handles of their cutlasses with a firm hand, ready to unsheathe them at the first intimation of alarm.

At the suggestion of the boatswain, who hinted at the necessity of having cleared decks, Captain de Haldimar had prevailed on his unfortunate relatives to retire to the small cabin arranged for their reception; and here they were attended by an aged female, who had long followed the fortunes of the crew, and acted in the twofold character of laundress and sempstress. He himself, with Sir Everard, continued on deck watching the progress of the vessel with an anxiety that became more intense at each succeeding hour. Hitherto their course had been unimpeded, save by the obstacles already enumerated; and they had now, at about an hour before dawn, gained a point that promised a speedy termination to their dangers and perplexities. Before them lay a reach in the river, enveloped in more than ordinary gloom, produced by the continuous weaving of the tops of the overhanging trees; and in the perspective, a gleam of relieving light, denoting the near vicinity of the lake that lay at the opposite extremity of the Sinclair, whose name it also bore. This was the narrowest part of the river; and so approximate were its shores, that the vessel in her course could not fail to come in contact both with the obtruding foliage of the forest and the dense bullrushes skirting the edge of either bank.

"If we get safe through this here place," said the boatswain, in a rough whisper to his anxious and attentive auditors, "I think as how I'll venture to answer for the craft. I can see daylight dancing upon the lake already. Ten minutes more and she will be there." Then turning to the man at the helm,—"Keep her in the centre of the stream, Jim. Don't you see you're hugging the weather shore?"

"It would take the devil himself to tell which is the centre," growled the sailor, in the same suppressed tone. "One might steer with one's eyes shut in such a queer place as this and never be no worser off than with them open."

"Steady her helm, steady," rejoined Mullins, "it's as dark as pitch, to be sure, but the passage is straight as an arrow, and with a steady helm you can't miss it. Make for the light ahead."

"Abaft there!" hurriedly and loudly shouted the man on the look-out at the bows, "there's a tree lying across the river, and we're just upon it."

While he yet spoke, and before the boatswain could give such instructions as the emergency required, the vessel suddenly struck against the obstacle in question; but the concussion was not of the violent nature that might have been anticipated. The course of the schooner, at no one period particularly rapid, had been considerably checked since her entrance into the gloomy arch, in the centre of which her present accident had occurred; so that it was without immediate injury to her hull and spars she had been thus suddenly brought to. But this was not the most alarming part of the affair. Captain de Haldimar and Sir Everard both recollected, that, in making the same passage, not forty-eight hours previously, they had encountered no obstacle of the kind, and a misgiving of danger rose simultaneously to the hearts of each. It was, however, a thing of too common occurrence in these countries, where storm and tempest were so prevalent and partial, to create more than a mere temporary alarm; for it was quite as probable the barrier had been interposed by some fitful outburst of Nature, as that it arose from design on the part of their enemies: and when the vessel had continued stationary for some minutes, without the prepared and expectant crew discovering the slightest indication of attack, the former impression was preserved by the officers—at least avowedly to those around.

"Bear a hand, my lads, and cut away," at length ordered the boatswain, in a low but clear tone; "half a dozen at each end of the stick, and we shall soon clear a passage for the craft."

A dozen sailors grasped their axes, and hastened forward to execute the command. They sprang lightly from the entangled bows of the schooner, and diverging in equal numbers moved to either extremity of the fallen tree.

"This is sailing through the heart of the American forest with a vengeance," muttered Mullins, whose annoyance at their detention was strongly manifested as he paced up and down the deck. "Shiver my topsails, if it isn't bad enough to clear the Sinclair at any time, much more so when one's running for one's life, and not a whisper's length from one's enemies. Do you know, Captain," abruptly checking his movement, and familiarly placing his hand on the shoulder of De Haldimar, "the last time we sailed through this very reach I couldn't help telling poor Captain Danvers, God rest his soul, what a nice spot it was for an Ingian ambuscade, if they had only gumption enough to think of it."

"Hark!" said the officer, whose heart, eye, and ear were painfully on the alert, "what rustling is that we hear overhead?"

"It's Jack Fuller, no doubt, your honour; I sent him up to clear away the branches from the main topmast rigging." Then raising his head, and elevating his voice, "Hilloa! aloft there!"

The only answer was a groan, followed by a deeper commotion among the rustling foliage.

"Why, what the devil's the matter with you now, Jack?" pursued the boatswain, in a voice of angry vehemence. "Are ye scared at another ghost, and be damned to you, that ye keep groaning there after that fashion?"

At that moment a heavy dull mass was heard tumbling through the upper rigging of the schooner towards the deck, and presently a human form fell at the very feet of the small group, composed of the two officers and the individual who had last spoken.

"A light, a light!" shouted the boatswain; "the foolish chap has lost his hold through fear, and ten to one if he hasn't cracked his skull-piece for his pains. Quick there with a light, and let's see what we can do for him."

The attention of all had been arrested by the sound of the falling weight, and as one of the sailors now advanced, bearing a dark lantern from below, the whole of the crew, with the exception of those employed on the fallen tree, gathered themselves in a knot round the motionless form of the prostrate man. But no sooner had their eyes encountered the object of their interest, when each individual started suddenly and involuntarily back, baring his cutlass, and drawing forth his pistol, the whole presenting a group of countenances strongly marked by various shades of consternation and alarm, even while their attitudes were those of men prepared for some fierce and desperate danger. It was indeed Fuller whom they had beheld, but not labouring, as the boatswain had imagined, under the mere influence of superstitious fear. He was dead, and the blood flowing from a deep wound, inflicted by a sharp instrument in his chest, and the scalped head, too plainly told the manner of his death, and the danger that awaited them all.

A pause ensued, but it was short. Before any one could find words to remark on the horrible circumstance, the appalling war-cry of the savages burst loudly from every quarter upon the ears of the devoted crew. In the desperation of the

41

moment, several of the men clutched their cutlasses between their teeth, and seizing the concealed matches, rushed to their respective stations at the guns. It was in vain the boatswain called out to them, in a voice of stern authority, to desist, intimating that their only protection lay in the reservation of the fire of their batteries. Goaded and excited, beyond the power of resistance, to an impulse that set all subordination at defiance, they applied the matches, and almost at the same instant the terrific discharge of both broadsides took place, rocking the vessel to the water's edge, and reverberating, throughout, the confined space in which she lay, like the deadly explosion of some deeply excavated mine.

Scarcely had the guns been fired, when the seamen became sensible of their imprudence. The echoes were yet struggling to force a passage through the dense forest, when a second yell of the Indians announced the fiercest joy and triumph, unmixed by disaster, at the result; and then the quick leaping of many forms could be heard, as they divided the crashing underwood, and rushed forward to close with their prey. It was evident, from the difference of sound, their first cry had been pealed forth while lying prostrate on the ground, and secure from the bullets, whose harmless discharge that cry was intended to provoke; for now the voices seemed to rise progressively from the earth, until they reached the level of each individual height, and were already almost hotly breathing in the ears of those they were destined to fill with illimitable dismay.

"Shiver my topsails, but this comes of disobeying orders," roared the boatswain, in a voice of mingled anger and vexation. "The Ingians are quite as cunning as ourselves, and arn't to be frighted that way. Quick, every cutlass and pistol to his gangway, and let's do our best. Pass the word forward for the axemen to return to quarters."

Recovered from their first paroxysm of alarm, the men at length became sensible of the presence of a directing power, which, humble as it was, their long habits of discipline had taught them to respect, and, headed on the one side by Captain de Haldimar, and on the other by Sir Everard Valletort, neither of whom, however, entertained the most remote chance of success, flew, as commanded, to their respective gangways. The yell of the Indians had again ceased, and all was hushed into stillness; but as the anxious and quicksighted officers gazed over the bulwarks, they fancied they could perceive, even through the deep gloom that every where prevailed, the forms of men,—resting in cautious and eager attitudes, on the very verge of the banks, and at a distance of little more than half pistol shot. Every heart beat with expectancy,—every eye was riveted intently in front, to watch and meet the first movements of their foes, but not a sound of approach was audible to the equally attentive ear. In this state of aching suspense they might

43

have continued about five minutes, when suddenly their hearts were made to quail by a third cry, that came, not as previously, from the banks of the river, but from the very centre of their own decks, and from the top-mast and riggings of the schooner. So sudden and unexpected too was this fresh danger, that before the two parties had time to turn, and assume a new posture of defence, several of them had already fallen under the butchering blades of their enemies. Then commenced a desperate but short conflict, mingled with yellings, that again were answered from every point; and rapidly gliding down the pendant ropes, were to be seen the active and dusky forms of men, swelling the number of the assailants, who had gained the deck in the same noiseless manner, until resistance became almost hopeless.

"Ha! I hear the footsteps of our lads at last," exclaimed Mullins exultingly to his comrades, as he finished despatching a third savage with his sturdy weapon. "Quick, men, quick, up with hatchet and cutlass, and take them in the rear. If we are to die, let's die—" game, he would perhaps have added, but death arrested the word upon his lips; and his corpse rolled along the deck, until its further progress was stopped by the stiffened body of the unhappy Fuller.

Notwithstanding the fall of their brave leader, and the whoopings of their enemies, the flagging spirits of the men were for a moment excited by the announcement of the return even of the small force of the axemen, and they defended themselves with a courage and determination worthy of a better result; but when, by the lurid light of the torches, now lying burning about the decks, they turned and beheld not their companions, but a fresh band of Indians, at whose pouch-belts dangled the reeking scalps of their murdered friends, they at once relinquished the combat as hopeless, and gave themselves unresistingly up to be bound by their captors.

Meanwhile the cousins experienced a renewal of all those horrors from which their distracted minds had been temporarily relieved; and, petrified with alarm, as they lay in the solitary berth that contained them both, endured sufferings infinitely more terrible than death itself. The early part of the tumult they had noticed almost without comprehending its cause, and but for the terrific cry of the Indians that had preceded them, would have mistaken the deafening broadsides for the blowing up of the vessel, so tremendous and violent bad been the concussion. Nay, there was a moment when Miss de Haldimar felt a pang of deep disappointment and regret at the misconception; for, with the fearful recollection of past events, so strongly impressed on her bleeding heart, she could not but acknowledge, that to be engulfed in one general and disastrous explosion, was mercy compared with the alternative of falling into the hands of those to whom her loathing spirit bad been too fatally taught to deny even the commonest attributes of humanity. As for Clara, she had not the power to think, or to form a conjecture on the subject:—she was merely sensible of a repetition of the horrible scenes from which she had so recently been snatched, and with a pale cheek, a fixed eye, and an almost pulseless heart, lay without motion in the inner side of the berth. The piteous spectacle of her cousin's alarm lent a forced activity to the despair of Miss de Haldimar, in whom apprehension produced that strong energy of excitement that sometimes gives to helplessness the character of true courage. With the increasing clamour of appalling conflict on deck, this excitement grew at every moment stronger, until it finally became irrepressible, so that at length, when through the cabin windows there suddenly streamed a flood of yellow light, extinguishing that of the lamp that threw its flickering beams around the cabin, she flung herself impetuously from the berth, and, despite of the aged and trembling female who attempted to detain her, burst open the narrow entrance to the cabin, and rushed up the steps communicating with the deck.

The picture that here met her eyes was at once graphic and fearful in the extreme. On either side of the river lines of streaming torches were waved by dusky warriors high above their heads, reflecting the grim countenances, not only of those who bore them, but of dense groups in their rear, whose numbers were alone concealed by the foliage of the forest in which they stood. From the branches that wove themselves across the centre of the river, and the topmast and rigging of the vessel, the same strong yellow light, produced by the bark of the birch tree steeped in gum, streamed down upon the decks below, rendering each line and block of the schooner as distinctly visible as if it had been noon on the sunniest of those far distant lakes. The deck itself was covered with the bodies of slain men— sailors, and savages mixed together; and amid these were to be seen fierce warriors, reclining triumphantly and indolently on their rifles, while others were occupied in securing the arms of their captives with leathern thongs behind their backs. The silence that now prevailed was strongly in contrast with, and even more fearful than, the horrid shouts by which it had been preceded; and, but for the ghastly countenances of the captives, and the quick rolling eyes of the savages, Miss de Haldimar might have imagined herself the sport of some extraordinary and exciting illusion. Her glance over these prominent features in the tragedy had been cursory, yet accurate. It now rested on one that had more immediate and terrifying interest for herself. At a few paces in front of the companion ladder, and with their backs turned towards her, stood two individuals, whose attitudes denoted the purpose of men resolved to sell with their lives alone a passage to a tall fierce-looking savage, whose countenance betrayed every mark of triumphant and deadly passion, while he apparently

47

hesitated whether his uplifted arm should stay the weapon it wielded. These individuals were Captain de Haldimar and Sir Everard Valletort; and to the former of these the attention of the savage was more immediately and exultingly directed; so much so, indeed, that Miss de Haldimar thought she could read in the ferocious expression of his features the death-warrant of her cousin. In the wild terror of the moment she gave a piercing scream that was answered by a hundred yelling voices, and rushing between her lover and his enemy, threw herself wildly and supplicatingly at the feet of the latter. Uttering a savage laugh, the monster spurned her from him with his foot, when, quick as thought, a pistol was discharged within a few inches of his face; but with a rapidity equal to that of his assailant, he bent aside his head, and the ball passed harmlessly on. The yell that followed was terrific; and while it was yet swelling into fulness, Captain de Haldimar felt an iron hand furiously grappling his throat, and, ere the grasp was relinquished, he again stood the bound and passive victim of the warrior of the Fleur de lis.

CHAPTER III.

The interval that succeeded to the last council-scene of the Indians was passed by the officers of Detroit in a state of inexpressible anxiety and doubt. The fears entertained for the fate of their companions, who had set out in the perilous and almost forlorn hope of reaching Michilimackinac, in time to prevent the consummation of the threatened treachery, had, in some degree, if not wholly, been allayed by the story narrated by the Ottawa chief. It was evident, from his statement, the party had again met, and been engaged in fearful struggle with the gigantic warrior they had all so much reason to recollect; and it was equally apparent, that in that struggle they had been successful. But still, so many obstacles were likely to be opposed to their navigation of the several lakes and rivers over which lay their course, it was almost feared, even if they eventually escaped unharmed themselves, they could not possibly reach the fort in time to communicate the danger that awaited their friends. It is true, the time gained by Governor de Haldimar on the first occasion had afforded a considerable interval, of which advantage might be taken; but it was also, on the other hand, uncertain whether Ponteac had commanded the same delay in the council of the chiefs investing Michilimackinac, to which he had himself assented. Three days were sufficient to enable an Indian warrior to perform the journey by land; and it was chiefly on this vague and uncertain ground they based whatever little of hope was entertained on the subject.

It had been settled at the departure of the adventurers, that the instant they effected a communication with the schooner on Lake Huron, Francois should be immediately sent back, with instructions so to contrive the period of his return, that his canoe should make its appearance soon after daybreak at the nearest extremity of Hog Island, the position of which has been described in our introductory chapter. From this point a certain signal, that could be easily distinguished with the aid of a telescope, was to be made from the canoe, which, without being of a nature to attract the attention of the savages, was yet to be such as could not well be mistaken by the garrison. This was a precaution adopted, not only with the view of giving the earliest intimation of the result of the enterprise, but lest the Canadian should be prevented, by any closer investment on the part of the Indians, from communicating personally with the fort in the way he had been accustomed.

It will easily be comprehended therefore, that, as the period approached when they might reasonably look for the return of Francois, if he should return at all, the nervous anxiety of the officers became more and more developed. Upwards of a week had elapsed since the departure of their friends; and already, for the last day or two, their impatience had led them, at early dawn, and with beating hearts, to that quarter of the rampart which overlooked the eastern extremity of Hog Island. Hitherto, however, their eager watching had been in vain. As far as our recollection of the Canadian tradition of this story serves us, it must have been on the fourth night after the final discomfiture of the plans of

Ponteac, and the tenth from the departure of the adventurers, that the officers were assembled in the mess-room, partaking of the scanty and frugal supper to which their long confinement had reduced them. The subject of their conversation, as it was ever of their thoughts, was the probable fate of their companions; and many and various, although all equally melancholy, were the conjectures offered as to the result. There was on the countenance of each, that deep and fixed expression of gloom, which, if it did not indicate any unmanliness of despair, told at least that hope was nearly extinct: but more especially was this remarkable in the young but sadly altered Charles de Haldimar, who, with a vacant eye and a pre-occupied manner, seemed wholly abstracted from the scene before him.

All was silence in the body of the fort. The men off duty had long since retired to rest in their clothes, and only the "All's well!" of the sentinels was heard at intervals of a quarter of an hour, as the cry echoed from mouth to mouth in the line of circuit. Suddenly, however, between two of those intervals, and during a pause in the languid conversation of the officers, the sharp challenge of a sentinel was heard, and then quick steps on the rampart, as of men hastening to the point whence the challenge had been given. The officers, whom this new excitement seemed to arouse into fresh activity, hurriedly quitted the room; and, with as little noise as possible, gained the spot where the voice had been heard. Several men were bending eagerly over the rampart, and, with their muskets at the recover, riveting their gaze on a dark and motionless object that lay on the verge of the ditch immediately beneath them.

"What have you here, Mitchell?" asked Captain Blessington, who was in command of the guard, and who had recognised the gruff voice of the veteran in the challenge just given.

"An American burnt log, your honour," muttered the soldier, "if one was to judge from its stillness; but if it is, it must have rolled there within the last minute; for I'll take my affidavy it wasn't here when I passed last in my beat."

"An American burnt log, indeed! it's some damned rascal of a spy, rather," remarked Captain Erskine. "Who knows but it may be our big friend, come to pay us a visit again? And yet he is not half long enough for him, either. Can't you try and tickle him with the bayonet, any of you fellows, and see whether he is made of flesh and blood?"

Although this observation was made almost without object, it being totally impossible for any musket, even with the addition of its bayonet, to reach more than half way across the ditch, the several sentinels threw themselves on their chests, and, stretching over the rampart as far as possible, made the attempt to reach the suspicious looking object that lay beyond. No sooner, however, had their arms been extended in such a manner as to be utterly powerless, when the dark mass was seen to roll away in an opposite direction, and with such rapidity that, before the men could regain their feet and level their muskets, it had entirely disappeared from their view.

"Cleverly managed, to give the red skin his due," half laughingly observed Captain Erskine, while his brother officers continued to fix their eyes in astonishment on the spot so recently occupied by the strange object; "but what the devil could be his motive for lying there so long? Not playing the eaves-dropper, surely; and yet, if he meant to have picked off a sentinel, what was to have prevented him from doing it sooner?"

"He had evidently no arms," said Ensign Delme.

"No, nor legs either, it would appear," resumed the literal Erskine. "Curse me if I ever saw any thing in the shape of a human form bundled together in that manner."

"I mean he had no fire-arms—no rifle," pursued Delme.

"And if he had, he certainly would have rifled one of us of a life," continued the captain, laughing at his own conceit. "But come, the bird is flown, and we have only to thank ourselves for having been so egregiously duped. Had Valletort been here, he would have given a different account of him."

53

"Hist! listen!" exclaimed Lieutenant Johnstone, calling the attention of the party to a peculiar and low sound in the direction in which the supposed Indian had departed.

It was repeated, and in a plaintive tone, indicating a desire to propitiate. Soon afterwards a human form was seen advancing slowly, but without show either of concealment or hostility in its movements. It finally remained stationary on the spot where the dark and shapeless mass had been first perceived.

"Another Oucanasta for De Haldimar, no doubt," observed Captain Erskine, after a moment's pause. "These grenadiers carry every thing before them as well in love as in war."

The error of the good-natured officer was, however, obvious to all but himself. The figure, which was now distinctly traced in outline for that of a warrior, stood boldly and fearlessly on the brink of the ditch, holding up its left arm, in the hand of which dangled something that was visible in the starlight, and pointing energetically to this pendant object with the other.

A voice from one of the party now addressed the Indian in two several dialects, but without eliciting a reply. He either understood not, or would not answer the question proposed, but continued pointing significantly to the indistinct object which he still held forth in an elevated position.

"The governor must be apprised of this," observed Captain Blessington to De Haldimar, who was his subaltern of the guard. "Hasten, Charles, to acquaint your father, and receive his orders."

The young officer willingly obeyed the injunction of his superior. A secret and indefinable hope rushed through his mind, that as the Indian came not in hostility, he might be the bearer of some communication from their friends; and he moved rapidly towards that part of the building occupied by his father.

The light of a lamp suspended over the piazza leading to the governor's rooms reflecting strongly on his regimentals, he passed unchallenged by the sentinels posted there, and uninterruptedly gained a door that opened on a narrow passage, at the further extremity of which was the sitting-room usually occupied by his parent. This again was entered from the same passage by a second door, the upper part of which was of common glass, enabling any one on the outside to trace with facility every object within when the place was lighted up.

A glance was sufficient to satisfy the youth his father was not in the room; although there was strong evidence he had not retired for the night. In the middle of the floor stood an oaken table, and on this lay an open writing desk, with a candle on each side, the wicks of which had burnt so long as to throw a partial gloom over the surrounding wainscotting. Scattered about the table and desk were a number of letters that had apparently been just looked at or read; and in the midst of these an open case of red morocco, containing a miniature. The appearance of these letters, thus left scattered about by one who was scrupulously exact in the arrangement of his papers, added to the circumstance of the neglected and burning candles, confirmed the young officer in an impression that his father, overcome by fatigue, had retired into his bed-room, and fallen unconsciously asleep. Imagining, therefore, he could not, without difficulty, succeed in making himself heard, and deeming the urgency of the case required it, he determined to wave the usual ceremony of knocking, and penetrate to his father's bedroom unannounced. The glass door being without fastening within, easily yielded to his pressure of the latch; but as he passed by the table, a strong and natural feeling of curiosity induced him to cast his eye upon the miniature. To his infinite surprise, nay, almost terror, he discovered it was that of his mother—the identical portrait which his sister Clara had worn in her bosom from infancy, and which he had seen clasped round her neck on the very deck of the schooner in which she sailed for Michilimackinac. He felt there could be no mistake, for only one miniature of the sort had ever been in possession of the family, and that the one just accounted for. Almost stupified at what he saw, and scarcely crediting the evidence of his senses, the young officer glanced his eye hurriedly along one of the open letters that lay around. It was in the well remembered handwriting of his mother, and commenced, "Dear, dearest Reginald." After this followed expressions of endearment no woman might address except to an affianced lover, or the husband of her choice; and his heart sickened while he read. Scarcely, however, had he scanned half a dozen lines, when it occurred to him he was violating some secret of his parents; and, discontinuing the perusal with an effort, he prepared to acquit himself of his mission.

On raising his eyes from the paper he was startled by the appearance of his father, who, with a stern brow and a quivering lip, stood a few paces from the table, apparently too much overcome by his indignation to be able to utter a sentence.

Charles de Haldimar felt all the awkwardness of his position. Some explanation of his conduct, however, was necessary; and he stammered forth the fact of the portrait having riveted his attention, from its striking resemblance to that in his sister's possession.

"And to what do these letters bear resemblance?" demanded the governor, in a voice that trembled in its attempt to be calm, while he fixed his penetrating eye on that of his son. "THEY, it appears, were equally objects of attraction with you."

"The letters were in the hand-writing of my mother; and I was irresistibly led to glance at one of them," replied the youth, with the humility of conscious wrong. "The action was involuntary, and no sooner committed than repented of. I am here, my father, on a mission of importance, which must account for my presence."

"A mission of importance!" repeated the governor, with more of sorrow than of anger in the tone in which he now spoke. "On what mission are you here, if it be not to intrude unwarrantably on a parent's privacy?"

The young officer's cheek flushed high, as he proudly answered:—"I was sent by Captain Blessington, sir, to take your orders in regard to an Indian who is now without the fort under somewhat extraordinary circumstances, yet evidently without intention of hostility. It is supposed he bears some message from my brother."

The tone of candour and offended pride in which this formal announcement of duty was made seemed to banish all suspicion from the mind of the governor; and he remarked, in a voice that had more of the kindness that had latterly distinguished his address to his son, "Was this, then, Charles, the only motive for your abrupt intrusion at this hour? Are you sure no inducement of private curiosity was mixed up with the discharge of your duty, that you entered thus unannounced? You must admit, at least, I found you employed in a manner different from what the urgency of your mission would seem to justify."

There was lurking irony in this speech; yet the softened accents of his father, in some measure, disarmed the youth of the bitterness he would have flung into his observation,—"That no man on earth, his parent excepted, should have dared to insinuate such a doubt with impunity."

For a moment Colonel de Haldimar seemed to regard his son with a surprised but satisfied air, as if he had not expected the manifestation of so much spirit, in one whom he had been accustomed greatly to undervalue.

"I believe you, Charles," he at length observed; "forgive the justifiable doubt, and think no more of the subject. Yet, one word," as the youth was preparing to depart; "you have read that letter" (and he pointed to that which had principally arrested the attention of the officer): "what impression has it given you of your mother? Answer me sincerely. MY name," and his faint smile wore something of the character of triumph, "is not REGINALD, you know."

The pallid cheek of the young man flushed at this question. His own undisguised impression was, that his mother had cherished a guilty love for another than her husband. He felt the almost impiety of such a belief, but he could not resist the conviction that forced itself on his mind; the letter in her handwriting spoke for itself; and though the idea was full of

59

wretchedness, he was unable to conquer it. Whatever his own inference might be, however, he could not endure the thought of imparting it to his father; he, therefore, answered evasively.

"Doubtless my mother had some dear relative of the name, and to him was this letter addressed; perhaps a brother, or an uncle. But I never knew," he pursued, with a look of appeal to his father, "that a second portrait of my mother existed. This is the very counterpart of Clara's."

"It may be the same," remarked the governor, but in a tone of indecision, that dented his faith in what he uttered.

"Impossible, my father. I accompanied Clara, if you recollect, as far as Lake Sinclair; and when I quitted the deck of the schooner to return, I particularly remarked my sister wore her mother's portrait, as usual, round her neck."

"Well, no matter about the portrait," hurriedly rejoined the governor; "yet, whatever your impression, Charles," and he spoke with a warmth that was far from habitual to him, "dare not to sully the memory of your mother by a doubt of her purity. An accident has given this letter to your inspection, but breathe not its contents to a human creature; above all, respect the being who gave you birth. Go, tell Captain Blessington to detain the Indian; I will join you immediately."

Strongly, yet confusedly, impressed with the singularity of the scene altogether, and more particularly with his father's strange admonition, the young officer quitted the room, and hastened to rejoin his companions. On reaching the rampart he found that the Indian, during his long absence, had departed; yet not without depositing, on the outer edge of the ditch, the substance to which he had previously directed their attention. At the moment of De Haldimar's approach, the officers were bending over the rampart, and, with straining eyes, endeavouring to make out what it was, but in vain; something was just perceptible in the withered turf, but what that something was no one could succeed in discovering.

"Whatever this be, we must possess ourselves of it," said Captain Blessington: "it is evident, from the energetic manner of him who left it, it is of importance. I think I know who is the best swimmer and climber of our party."

Several voices unanimously pronounced the name of "Johnstone."

"Any thing for a dash of enterprise," said that officer, whose slight wound had been perfectly healed. "But what do you propose that the swimmer and climber should do, Blessington?"

"Secure yon parcel, without lowering the drawbridge."

"What! and be scalped in the act? Who knows if it be not a trick after all, and that the rascal who placed it there is not lying within a few feet, ready to pounce upon me the instant I reach the bank."

"Never mind," said Erskine, laughingly, "we will revenge your death, my boy."

"Besides, consider the nunquam non paratus, Johnstone," slily remarked Lieutenant Leslie.

"What, again, Leslie?" energetically responded the young Scotsman. "Yet think not I hesitate, for I did but jest: make fast a rope round my loins, and I think I will answer for the result."

Colonel de Haldimar now made his appearance. Having heard a brief statement of the facts, and approving of the suggestion of Captain Blessington, a rope was procured, and made fast under the shoulders of the young officer, who had previously stripped himself of his uniform and shoes. He then suffered himself to drop gently over the edge of the rampart, his companions gradually lowering the rope, until a deep and gasping aspiration, such as is usually wrung from one coming suddenly in contact with cold water, announced he had gained the surface of the ditch. The rope was then slackened, to give him the unrestrained command of his limbs; and in the next instant he was seen clambering up the opposite elevation.

Although the officers, indulging in a forced levity, in a great degree meant to encourage their companion, had treated his enterprise with indifference, they were far from being without serious anxiety for the result. They had laughed at the idea, suggested by him, of being scalped; whereas, in truth, they entertained the apprehension far more powerfully than he did himself. The artifices resorted to by the savages, to secure an isolated victim, were so many and so various, that suspicion could not but attach to the mysterious occurrence they had just witnessed. Willing even as they were to believe their present visitor, whoever he was, came not in a spirit of enmity, they could not altogether divest themselves of a fear that it was only a subtle artifice to decoy one of them within the reach of their traitorous weapons. They, therefore, watched the movements of their companion with quickening pulses; and it was with a lively satisfaction they saw him, at length, after a momentary search, descend once more into the ditch, and, with a single powerful impulsion of his limbs, urge himself back to the foot of the rampart. Neither feet nor hands were of much service, in enabling him to scale the smooth and slanting logs that composed the exterior surface of the works; but a slight jerk of the well secured rope, serving as a signal to his friends, he was soon dragged once more to the summit of the rampart, without other injury than a couple of slight bruises.

"Well, what success?" eagerly asked Leslie and Captain Erskine in the same breath, as the dripping Johnstone buried himself in the folds of a capacious cloak procured during his absence.

"You shall hear," was the reply; "but first, gentlemen, allow me, if you please, to enjoy, with yourselves, the luxury of dry clothes. I have no particular ambition to contract an American ague fit just now; yet, unless you take pity on me, and reserve my examination for a future moment, there is every probability I shall not have a tooth left by to-morrow morning."

No one could deny the justice of the remark, for the teeth of the young man were chattering as he spoke. It was not, therefore, until after he had changed his dress, and swallowed a couple of glasses of Captain Erskine's never failing spirit, that they all repaired once more to the mess-room, when Johnstone anticipated all questions, by the production of the mysterious packet.

After removing several wrappers of bark, each of which was secured by a thong of deerskin, Colonel de Haldimar, to whom the successful officer had handed his prize, at length came to a small oval case of red morocco, precisely similar, in size and form, to that which had so recently attracted the notice of his son. For a moment he hesitated, and his cheek was observed to turn pale, and his hand to tremble; but quickly subduing his indecision, he hurriedly unfastened the clasp, and disclosed to the astonished view of the officers the portrait of a young and lovely woman, habited in the Highland garb.

Exclamations of various kinds burst from the lips of the group of officers. Several knew it to be the portrait of Mrs. de Haldimar; others recognised it from the striking likeness it bore to Clara and to Charles; all knew it had never been absent from the possession of the former since her mother's death; and feeling satisfied as they did that its extraordinary appearance among them, at the present moment, was an announcement of some dreadful disaster, their countenances wore an impress of dismay little inferior to that of the wretched Charles, who, agonized beyond all attempt at description, had thrown himself into a seat in the rear of the group, and sat like one bewildered, with his head buried in his hands.

"Gentlemen," at length observed Colonel de Haldimar, in a voice that proved how vainly his natural emotion was sought to be subdued by his pride, "this, I fear me, is an unwelcome token. It comes to announce to a father the murder of his child; to us all, the destruction of our last remaining friends and comrades."

"God forbid!" solemnly aspirated Captain Blessington. After a pause of a moment or two he pursued: "I know not why, sir; but my impression is, the appearance of this portrait, which we all recognise for that worn by Miss de Haldimar, bears another interpretation."

Colonel de Haldimar shook his head.—"I have but too much reason to believe," he observed, smiling in mournful bitterness, "it has been conveyed to us not in mercy but in revenge."

No one ventured to question why; for notwithstanding all were aware that in the mysterious ravisher of the wife of Halloway Colonel de Haldimar had a fierce and inexorable private enemy, no allusion had ever been made by that officer himself to the subject.

"Will you permit me to examine the portrait and envelopes, Colonel?" resumed Captain Blessington: "I feel almost confident, although I confess I have no other motive for it than what springs from a recollection of the manner of the Indian, that the result will bear me out in my belief the bearer came not in hostility but in friendship."

"By my faith, I quite agree with Blessington," said Captain Erskine; "for, in addition to the manner of the Indian, there is another evidence in favour of his position. Was it merely intended in the light in which you consider it, Colonel, the case or the miniature itself might have been returned, but certainly not the metal in which it is set. The savages are fully aware of the value of gold, and would not so easily let it slip through their fingers."

"And wherefore thus carefully wrapped up?" remarked Lieutenant Johnstone, "unless it had been intended it should meet with no injury on the way. I certainly think the portrait never would have been conveyed, in its present perfect state, by an enemy."

"The fellow seemed to feel, too, that he came in the character of one whose intentions claimed all immunity from harm," remarked Captain Wentworth. "He surely never would have stood so fearlessly on the brink of the ditch, and within pistol shot, had he not been conscious of rendering some service to those connected with us."

To these several observations of his officers, Colonel de Haldimar listened attentively; and although he made no reply, it was evident he felt gratified at the eagerness with which each sought to remove the horrible impression he had stated to have existed in his own mind. Meanwhile, Captain Blessington had turned and examined the miniature in fifty different ways, but without succeeding in discovering any thing that could confirm him in his original impression. Vexed and disappointed, he at length flung it from him on the table, and sinking into a seat at the side of the unfortunate Charles, pressed the hand of the youth in significant silence.

Finding his worst fears now confirmed. Colonel de Haldimar, for the first time, cast a glance towards his son, whose drooping head, and sorrowing attitude, spoke volumes to his heart. For a moment his own cheek blanched, and his eye was seen to glisten with the first tear ever witnessed there by those around him. Subduing his emotion, however, he drew up his person to its lordly height, as if that act reminded him the commander was not to be lost in the father, and quitting the room with a heavy brow and step, recommended to his officers the repose of which they appeared to stand so much in need. But not one was there who felt inclined to court the solitude of his pillow. No sooner were the footsteps of the governor heard dying away in the distance, when fresh lights were ordered, and several logs of wood heaped on the slackening fire. Around this the officers now grouped, and throwing themselves back in their chairs, assumed the attitudes of men seeking to indulge rather in private reflection than in personal converse.

The grief of the wretched Charles de Haldimar, hitherto restrained by the presence of his father, and encouraged by the touching evidences of interest afforded him by the ever-considerate Blessington, now burst forth audibly. No attempt was made by the latter officer to check the emotion of his young friend. Knowing his passionate fondness for his sister, he was not without fear that the sudden shock produced by the appearance of her miniature might destroy his reason, even if it affected not his life; and as the moment was now come when tears might be shed without exciting invidious remark in the only individual who was likely to make it, he sought to promote them as much as possible. Too much occupied in their own mournful reflections to bestow more than a passing notice on the weakness of their friend, the group round the fireplace scarcely seemed to have regarded his emotion.

This violent paroxysm past, De Haldimar breathed more freely; and, after listening to several earnest observations of Captain Blessington, who still held out the possibility of something favourable turning up, on a re-examination of the portrait by daylight, he was so far composed as to be able to attend to the summons of the sergeant of the guard, who came to say the relief were ready, and waiting to be inspected before they were finally marched off. Clasping the extended hand of his captain between his own, with a pressure indicative of his deep gratitude, De Haldimar now proceeded to the discharge of his duty; and having caught up the portrait, which still lay on the table, and thrust it into the breast of his uniform, he repaired hurriedly to rejoin his guard, from which circumstances alone had induced his unusually long absence.

CHAPTER IV.

The remainder of that night was passed by the unhappy De Haldimar in a state of indescribable wretchedness. After inspecting the relief, he had thrown himself on his rude guard-bed; and, drawing his cloak over his eyes, given full rein to the wanderings of his excited imagination. It was in vain the faithful old Morrison, who never suffered his master to mount a guard without finding some one with whom to exchange his tour of duty, when he happened not to be in orders himself, repeatedly essayed, as he sat stirring the embers of the fire, to enter into conversation with him. The soul of the young officer was sick, past the endurance even of that kind voice; and, more than once, he impetuously bade him be silent, if he wished to continue where he was; or, if not, to join his comrades in the next guard-room. A sigh was the only respectful but pained answer to these sharp remonstrances; and De Haldimar, all absorbed even as he was in his own grief, felt it deeply; for he knew the old man loved him, and he could not bear the idea of appearing to repay with slight the well-intentioned efforts of one whom he had always looked upon more as a dependant on his family than as the mere rude soldier. Still he could not summon courage to disclose the true nature of his grief, which the other merely ascribed to general causes and vague apprehensions of a yet unaccomplished evil. Morrison had

70

ever loved his sister with an affection in no way inferior to that which he bore towards himself. He had also nursed her in childhood; and his memory was ever faithful to trace, as his tongue was to dwell on, those gentle and amiable qualities, which, strongly marked at an earlier period of her existence, had only undergone change, inasmuch as they had become matured and more forcibly developed in womanhood. Often, latterly, had the grey-haired veteran been in the habit of alluding to her; for he saw the subject was one that imparted a mournful satisfaction to the youth; and, with a tact that years, more than deep reading of the human heart, had given him, he ever made a point of adverting to their re-union as an event admitting not of doubt.

Hitherto the affectionate De Haldimar had loved to listen to these sounds of comfort; for, although they carried no conviction to his mind, impressed as he was with the terrible curse of Ellen Halloway, and the consequent belief that his family were devoted to some fearful doom, still they came soothingly and unctuously to his sick soul; and, all deceptive even as he felt them to be, he found they created a hope which, while certain to be dispelled by calm after-reflection, carried a momentary solace to his afflicted spirit. But, now that he had every evidence his adored sister was no more, and that the illusion of hope was past for ever, to have heard her name even mentioned by one who, ignorant of the

71

fearful truth the events of that night had elucidated, was still ready to renew a strain every chord of which had lost its power of harmony, was repugnant beyond bearing to his heart. At one moment he resolved briefly to acquaint the old man with the dreadful fact, but unwillingness to give pain prevented him; and, moreover, he felt the grief the communication would draw from the faithful servitor of his family must be of so unchecked a nature as to render his own sufferings even more poignant than they were. Neither had he (independently of all other considerations) resolution enough to forego the existence of hope in another, even although it had passed entirely away from himself. It was for these reasons he had so harshly and (for him) unkindly checked, the attempt of the old man at a conversation which he, at every moment, felt would be made to turn on the ill-fated Clara.

Miserable as he felt his position to be, it was not without satisfaction he again heard the voice of his sergeant summoning him to the inspection of another relief. This duty performed, and anxious to avoid the paining presence of his servant, he determined, instead of returning to his guard-room, to consume the hour that remained before day in pacing the ramparts. Leaving word with his subordinate, that, in the event of his being required, he might be found without difficulty, he ascended to that quarter of the works where the Indian had been first seen who had so mysteriously conveyed the sad token he still retained in his breast. It was on the same side with that particular point whence we have already stated a full view of the bridge with its surrounding scenery, together with the waters of the Detroit, where they were intersected by Hog Island, were distinctly commanded. At either of those points was stationed a sentinel, whose duty it was to extend his beat between the boxes used now rather as lines of demarcation than as places of temporary shelter, until each gained that of his next comrade, when they again returned to their own, crossing each other about half way: a system of precaution pursued by the whole of the sentinels in the circuit of the rampart.

The ostensible motive of the officer in ascending the works, was to visit his several posts; but no sooner had he found himself between the points alluded to, which happened to be the first in his course, than he seemed to be riveted there by a species of fascination. Not that there was any external influence to produce this effect, for the utmost stillness reigned both within and around the fort; and, but for the howling of some Indian wolf-dog in the distance, or the low and monotonous beat of their drums in the death-dance, there was nought that gave evidence of the existence of the dreadful enemy by whom they were beset. But the whole being of the acutely suffering De Haldimar was absorbed in recollections connected with the spot on which he stood. At one extremity was the point whence he had witnessed the dreadful tragedy of Halloway's death; at the other, that on which had been deposited the but too unerring record of the partial realisation of the horrors threatened at the termination of that tragedy; and whenever he attempted to pass each of these boundaries, he felt as if his limbs repugned the effort.

In the sentinels, his appearance among them excited but little surprise; for it was no uncommon thing for the officers of the guard to spend the greatest part of the night in visiting, in turn, the several more exposed points of the ramparts; and that it was now confined to one particular part, seemed not even to attract their notice. It was, therefore, almost wholly unremarked by his men, that the heart-stricken De Haldimar paced his quick and uncertain walk with an imagination filled with the most fearful forebodings, and with a heart throbbing with the most painful excitement. Hitherto, since the discovery of the contents of the packet, his mind had been so exclusively absorbed in stupifying grief for his sister, that his perception seemed utterly incapable of outstepping the limited sphere drawn around it; but now, other remembrances, connected with the localities, forced themselves upon his attention; and although, in all these, there was nothing that was not equally calculated to carry dismay and sorrow to his heart, still, in dividing his thoughts with the one supreme agony that bowed him down, they were rather welcomed than discarded. His mind was as a wheel, embracing grief within grief, multiplied to infinitude; and the wider and more diffusive the circle, the less powerful was the concentration of sickening heart and brain on that which was the more immediate axis of the whole.

Reminded, for the first time, as he pursued his measured but aimless walk, by the fatal portrait which he more than once pressed with feverish energy to his lips, of the singular discovery he had made that night in the apartments of his father, he was naturally led, by a chain of consecutive thought, into a review of the whole of the extraordinary scene. The fact of the existence of a second likeness of his mother was one that did not now fail to reawaken all the unqualified surprise he had experienced at the first discovery. So far from having ever heard his father make the slightest allusion to this memorial of his departed mother, he perfectly recollected his repeatedly recommending to Clara the safe custody of a treasure, which, if lost, could never be replaced. What could be the motive for this mystery?—and why had he sought to impress him with the belief it was the identical portrait worn by his sister which had so unintentionally been exposed to his view? Why, too, had he evinced so much anxiety to remove from his mind all unfavourable impressions in regard to his mother? Why have been so energetic in his caution not to suffer a taint of impurity to attach to her memory? Why should he have supposed the possibility of such impression, unless there had been sufficient cause for it? In what, moreover, originated his triumphant expression of feature, when, on that occasion, he reminded him that HIS name was not Reginald? Who, then, was this Reginald? Then came the recollection of what had been repeated to him of the parting scene between Halloway and his wife. In addressing her ill-fated husband, she had named him Reginald. Could it be possible this was the same being alluded to by his father? But no; his youth forbade the supposition, being but two years older than his brother Frederick; yet might he not, in some way or other, be connected with the Reginald of the letter? Why, too, had his father shown such unrelenting severity in the case of this unfortunate victim?—a severity which had induced more than one remark from his officers, that it looked as if he entertained some personal feeling of enmity towards a man who had done so much for his family, and stood so high in the esteem of all who knew him.

Then came another thought. At the moment of his execution, Halloway had deposited a packet in the hands of Captain Blessington;—could these letters—could that portrait be the same? Certain it was, by whatever means obtained, his father could not have had them long in his possession; for it was improbable letters of so old a date should have occupied his attention NOW, when many years had rolled over the memory of his mother. And then, again, what was the meaning of the language used by the implacable enemy of his father, that uncouth and ferocious warrior of the Fleur de lis, not only on the occasion of the execution of Halloway, but afterwards to his brother, during his short captivity; and, subsequently, when, disguised as a black, he penetrated, with the band of Ponteac, into the fort, and aimed his murderous weapon at his father's head. What had made him the enemy of his family? and where and how had originated his father's connection with so extraordinary and so savage a being? Could he, in any way, be implicated with his mother? But no; there was something revolting, monstrous, in the thought: besides, had not his father stood forward the champion of her innocence?—had he not declared, with an energy carrying conviction with every word, that she was untainted by guilt? And would he have done this, had he had reason to believe in the existence of a criminal love for him who evidently was his mortal foe? Impossible.

Such were the questions and solutions that crowded on and distracted the mind of the unhappy De Haldimar, who, after all, could arrive at no satisfactory conclusion. It was evident there was a secret,—yet, whatever its nature, it was one likely to go down with his father to the grave; for, however humiliating the reflection to a haughty parent, compelled to vindicate the honour of a mother to her son, and in direct opposition to evidence that scarcely bore a shadow of misinterpretation, it was clear he had motives for consigning the circumstance to oblivion, which far outweighed any necessity he felt of adducing other proofs of her innocence than those which rested on his own simple yet impressive assertion.

In the midst of these bewildering doubts, De Haldimar heard some one approaching in his rear, whose footsteps he distinguished from the heavy pace of the sentinels. He turned, stopped, and was presently joined by Captain Blessington.

"Why, dearest Charles," almost querulously asked the kind officer, as he passed his arm through that of his subaltern,— "why will you persist in feeding this love of solitude? What possible result can it produce, but an utter prostration of every moral and physical energy? Come, come, summon a little fortitude; all may not yet be so hopeless as you apprehend. For my own part, I feel convinced the day will dawn upon some satisfactory solution of the mystery of that packet."

"Blessington, my dear Blessington!"—and De Haldimar spoke with mournful energy,—"you have known me from my boyhood, and, I believe, have ever loved me; seek not, therefore, to draw me from the present temper of my mind;

deprive me not of an indulgence which, melancholy as it is, now constitutes the sole satisfaction I take in existence."

"By Heaven! Charles, I will not listen to such language. You absolutely put my patience to the rack."

"Nay, then, I will urge no more," pursued the young officer. "To revert, therefore, to a different subject. Answer me one question with sincerity. What were the contents of the packet you received from poor Halloway previous to his execution? and in whose possession are they now?"

Pleased to find the attention of his young friend diverted for the moment from his sister, Captain Blessington quickly rejoiced, he believed the packet contained letters which Halloway had stated to him were of a nature to throw some light on his family connections. He had, however, transferred it, with the seal unbroken, as desired by the unhappy man, to Colonel de Haldimar.

An exclamation of surprise burst involuntarily from the lips of the youth. "Has my father ever made any allusion to that packet since?" he asked.

"Never," returned Captain Blessington; "and, I confess, his failing to do so has often excited my astonishment. But why do you ask?"

De Haldimar energetically pressed the arm of his captain, while a heavy sigh burst from his oppressed heart "This very night, Blessington, on entering my father's apartment to apprise him of what was going on here, I saw,—I can scarcely tell you what, but certainly enough to convince me, from what you have now stated, Halloway was, in some degree or other, connected with our family. Tell me," he anxiously pursued, "was there a portrait enclosed with the letters?"

"I cannot state with confidence, Charles," replied his friend; "but if I might judge from the peculiar form and weight of the packet, I should be inclined to say not. Have you seen the letters, then?"

"I have seen certain letters which, I have reason to believe, are the same," returned De Haldimar. "They were addressed to 'Reginald;' and Halloway, I think you have told me, was so called by his unhappy wife."

"There can be little doubt they are the same," said Captain Blessington; "but what were their contents, and by whom written, that you deem they prove a connection between the unhappy soldier and your family?"

De Haldimar felt the blood rise into his cheek, at this natural but unexpected demand. "I am sure, Blessington," he replied, after a pause, "you will not think me capable of unworthy mystery towards yourself but the contents of these letters are sacred, inasmuch as they relate only to circumstances connected with my father's family."

"This is singular indeed," exclaimed Captain Blessington, in a tone that marked his utter and unqualified astonishment at what had now been disclosed to him; "but surely, Charles," he pursued, "if the packet handed me by Halloway were the same you allude to, he would have caused the transfer to have been made before the period chosen by him for that purpose."

"But the name," pursued De Haldimar; "how are we to separate the identity of the packets, when we recur to that name of 'Reginald?'"

"True," rejoined the musing Blessington; "there is a mystery in this that baffles all my powers of penetration. Were I in possession of the contents of the letters, I might find some clue to solve the enigma: but—"

"You surely do not mean this as a reproach, Blessington?" fervently interrupted the youth. "More I dare not, cannot say, for the secret is not my own; and feelings, which it would be dishonour to outrage, alone bind me to silence. What little I have revealed to you even now, has been uttered in confidence. I hope you have so understood it."

"Perfectly, Charles. What you have stated, goes no further; but we have been too long absent from our guard, and I confess I have no particular fancy for remaining in this chill night-air. Let us return."

De Haldimar made no opposition, and they both prepared to quit the rampart. As they passed the sentinel stationed at that point where the Indian had been first seen, their attention was directed by him to a fire that now suddenly rose, apparently at a great distance, and rapidly increased in volume. The singularity of this occurrence riveted the officers for a moment in silent observation; until Captain Blessington at length ventured a remark, that, judging from the direction, and the deceptive nature of the element at night, he should incline to think it was the hut of the Canadian burning.

"Which is another additional proof, were any such wanting, that every thing is lost," mournfully urged the ever apprehensive De Haldimar. "Francois has been detected in rendering aid to our friends; and the Indians, in all probability, after having immolated their victim, are sacrificing his property to their rage."

During this exchange of opinions, the officers had again moved to the opposite point of the limited walk of the younger. Scarcely had they reached it, and before Captain Blessington could find time to reply to the fears of his friend, when a loud and distant booming like that of a cannon was heard in the direction of the fire. The alarm was given hastily by the sentinels, and sounds of preparation and arming were audible in the course of a minute or two every where throughout the fort. Startled by the report, which they had half inclined to imagine produced by the discharge of one of their own guns, the half slumbering officers had quitted the chairs in which they had passed the night in the mess-room, and were soon at the side of their more watchful companions, then anxiously listening for a repetition of the sound.

The day was just beginning to dawn, and as the atmosphere cleared gradually away, it was perceived the fire rose not from the hut of the Canadian, but at a point considerably beyond it. Unusual as it was to see a large fire of this description, its appearance became an object of minor consideration, since it might be attributed to some caprice or desire on the part of the Indians to excite apprehension in their enemies. But how was the report which had reached their ears to be accounted for? It evidently could only have been produced by the discharge of a cannon; and if so, where could the Indians have procured it? No such arm had recently been in their possession; and if it were, they were totally unacquainted with the manner of serving it.

As the day became more developed, the mystery was resolved. Every telescope in the fort had been called into requisition; and as they were now levelled in the direction of the fire, sweeping the line of horizon around, exclamations of surprise escaped the lips of several.

"The fire is at the near extremity of the wood on Hog Island," exclaimed Lieutenant Johnstone. "I can distinctly see the forms of a multitude of savages dancing round it with hideous gestures and menacing attitudes."

"They are dancing their infernal war dance," said Captain Wentworth. "How I should like to be able to discharge a twenty-four pound battery, loaded with grape, into the very heart of the devilish throng."

"Do you see any prisoners?—Are any of our friends among them?" eagerly and tremblingly enquired De Haldimar of the officer who had last spoken.

Captain Wentworth made a sweep of his glass along the shores of the island; but apparently without success. He announced that he could discover nothing but a vast number of bark canoes lying dry and upturned on the beach.

"It is an unusual hour for their war dance," observed Captain Blessington. "My experience furnishes me with no one instance in which it has not been danced previous to their retiring to rest."

"Unless," said Lieutenant Boyce, "they should have been thus engaged all night; in which case the singularity may be explained."

"Look, look," eagerly remarked Lieutenant Johnstone— "see how they are flying to their canoes, bounding and leaping like so many devils broke loose from their chains. The fire is nearly deserted already."

"The schooner—the schooner!" shouted Captain Erskine. "By Heaven, our own gallant schooner! see how beautifully she drives past the island. It was her gun we heard, intended as a signal to prepare us for her appearance."

A thrill of wild and indescribable emotion passed through every heart. Every eye was turned upon the point to which attention was now directed. The graceful vessel, with every stitch of canvass set, was shooting rapidly past the low bushes skirting the sands that still concealed her hull; and in a moment or two she loomed largely and proudly on the bosom of the Detroit, the surface of which was slightly curled with a north-western breeze.

"Safe, by Jupiter!" exclaimed the delighted Erskine, dropping the glass upon the rampart, and rubbing his hands together with every manifestation of joy.

"The Indians are in chase," said Lieutenant Boyce; "upwards of fifty canoes are following in the schooner's wake. But Danvers will soon give us an account of their Lilliputian fleet."

"Let the troops be held in readiness for a sortie, Mr. Lawson," said the governor, who had joined his officers just as the schooner cleared the island; "we must cover their landing, or, with this host of savages in pursuit, they will never effect it alive."

During the whole of this brief but exciting scene, the heart of Charles de Haldimar beat audibly. A thousand hopes and fears rushed confusedly on his mind, and he was as one bewildered by, and scarcely crediting what he saw. Could Clara,—could his cousin—could his brother—could his friend be on board? He scarcely dared to ask himself these questions; still it was with a fluttering heart, in which hope, however, predominated, that he hastened to execute an order of his captain, that bore immediate reference to his duty as subaltern of the guard.

CHAPTER V.

Meanwhile the schooner dashed rapidly along, her hull occasionally hid from the view of those assembled on the ramparts by some intervening orchard or cluster of houses, but her tall spars glittering in their covering of white canvass, and marking the direction of her course. At length she came to a point in the river that offered no other interruption to the eye than what arose from the presence of almost all the inhabitants of the village, who, urged by curiosity and surprise, were to be seen crowding the intervening bank. Here the schooner was suddenly put about, and the English colours, hitherto concealed by the folds of the canvass, were at length discovered proudly floating in the breeze.

Immediately over the gateway of the fort there was an elevated platform, approached by the rampart, of which it formed a part, by some half dozen rude steps on either side; and on this platform was placed a long eighteen pounder, that commanded the whole extent of road leading from the drawbridge to the river. Hither the officers had all repaired, while the schooner was in the act of passing the town; and now that, suddenly brought up in the wind's eye, she rode leisurely in the offing, every movement on her decks was plainly discernible with the telescope.

"Where the devil can Danvers have hid all his crew?" first spoke Captain Erskine; "I count but half a dozen hands altogether on deck, and these are barely sufficient to work her."

"Lying concealed, and ready, no doubt, to give the canoes a warm reception," observed Lieutenant Johnstone; "but where can our friends be? Surely, if there, they would show themselves to us."

There was truth in this remark; and each felt discouraged and disappointed that they did not appear.

"There come the whooping hell fiends," said Major Blackwater. "By Heaven! the very water is darkened with the shadows of their canoes."

Scarcely had he spoken, when the vessel was suddenly surrounded by a multitude of savages, whose fierce shouts rent the air, while their dripping paddles, gleaming like silver in the rays of the rising sun, were alternately waved aloft in triumph, and then plunged into the troubled element, which they spurned in fury from their blades.

"What can Danvers be about? Why does he not either open his fire, or crowd sail and away from them?" exclaimed several voices.

"The detachment is in readiness, sir," said Mr. Lawson, ascending the platform, and addressing Major Blackwater.

"The deck, the deck!" shouted Erskine.

Already the eyes of several were bent in the direction alluded to by the last speaker, while those whose attention had been diverted by the approaching canoes glanced rapidly to the same point. To the surprise and consternation of all, the tall and well-remembered form of the warrior of the Fleur de lis was seen towering far above the bulwarks of the schooner; and with an expression in the attitude he had assumed, which no one could mistake for other than that of triumphant defiance. Presently he drew from the bosom of his hunting coat a dark parcel, and springing into the rigging of the main-mast, ascended with incredible activity to the point where the English ensign was faintly floating in the breeze. This he tore furiously away, and rending it into many pieces, cast the fragments into the silver element beneath him, on whose bosom they were seen to float among the canoes of the savages, many of whom possessed themselves, with eagerness, of the gaudy coloured trophies. The dark parcel was now unfolded by the active warrior, who, after having waved it several times round his head, commenced attaching it to the lines whence the English ensign had so recently been torn. It was a large black flag, the purport of which was too readily comprehended by the excited officers.

"D—n the ruffian! can we not manage to make that, flag serve as his own winding sheet?" exclaimed Captain Erskine. "Come, Wentworth, give us a second edition of the sortie firing; I know no man who understands pointing a gun better than yourself, and this eighteen pounder might do some mischief."

The idea was instantly caught at by the officer of artillery, who read his consent in the eye of Colonel de Haldimar. His companions made way on either side; and several gunners, who were already at their stations, having advanced to work the piece at the command of their captain, it was speedily brought to bear upon the schooner.

"This will do, I think," said Wentworth, as, glancing his experienced eye carefully along the gun, he found it pointed immediately on the gigantic frame of the warrior. "If this chain-shot miss him, it will be through no fault of mine."

Every eye was now riveted on the main-mast of the schooner, where the warrior was still engaged in attaching the portentous flag. The gunner, who held the match, obeyed the silent signal of his captain; and the massive iron was heard rushing past the officers, bound on its murderous mission. A moment or two of intense anxiety elapsed; and when at length the rolling volumes of smoke gradually floated away, to the dismay and disappointment of all, the fierce warrior was seen standing apparently unharmed on the same spot in the rigging. The shot had, however, been well aimed, for a large rent in the outstretched canvass, close at his side, and about mid-height of his person, marked the direction it had taken. Again he tore away, and triumphantly waved the black flag around his head, while from his capacious lungs there burst yells of defiance and scorn, that could be distinguished for his own even at that distance. This done, he again secured the death symbol to its place; and gliding to the deck by a single rope, appeared to give orders to the few men of the crew who were to be seen; for every stitch of canvass was again made to fill, and the vessel, bounding forward before the breeze then blowing upon her quarter, shot rapidly behind the town, and was finally seen to cast anchor in the navigable channel that divides Hog Island from the shores of Canada.

At the discharge of the eighteen pounder, the river had been suddenly cleared, as if by magic, of every canoe; while, warned by the same danger, the groups of inhabitants, assembled on the bank, had rushed for shelter to their respective homes; so that, when the schooner disappeared, not a vestige of human life was to be seen along that vista so recently peopled with human forms. An order from Colonel de Haldimar to the adjutant, countermanding the sortie, was the first interruption to the silence that had continued to pervade the little band of officers; and two or three of these having hastened to the western front of the rampart, in order to obtain a more distinct view of the movements of the schooner, their example was speedily followed by the remainder, all of whom now quitted the platform, and repaired to the same point.

Here, with the aid of their telescopes, they again distinctly commanded a view of the vessel, which lay motionless close under the sandy beach of the island, and exhibiting all the technicalities of skill in the disposition of sails and yards peculiar to the profession. In vain, however, was every eye strained to discover, among the multitude of savages that kept momentarily leaping to her deck, the forms of those in whom they were most interested. A group of some half dozen men, apparently common sailors, and those, in all probability, whose services had been compelled in the working of the vessel, were the only evidences that civilised man formed a portion of that grotesque assemblage. These, with their arms evidently bound behind their backs, and placed on one of the gangways, were only visible at intervals, as the band of savages that surrounded them, brandishing their tomahawks around their heads, occasionally left an opening in their circle. The formidable warrior of the Fleur de lis was no longer to be seen, although the flag which he had hoisted still fluttered in the breeze.

"All is lost, then," ejaculated the governor, with a mournfulness of voice and manner that caused many of his officers to turn and regard him with surprise. "That black flag announces the triumph of my foe in the too certain destruction of my children. Now, indeed," he concluded in a lower tone, "for the first time, does the curse of Ellen Halloway sit heavily on my soul."

A deep sigh burst from one immediately behind him. The governor turned suddenly round, and beheld his son. Never did human countenance wear a character of more poignant misery than that of the unhappy Charles at the moment. Attracted by the report of the cannon, he had flown to the rampart to ascertain the cause, and had reached his companions only to learn the strong hope so recently kindled in his breast was fled for ever. His cheek, over which hung his neglected hair, was now pale as marble, and his lips bloodless and parted; yet, notwithstanding this intensity of personal sorrow, a tear had started to his eye, apparently wrung from him by this unusual expression of dismay in his father.

"Charles—my son—my only now remaining child," murmured the governor with emotion, as he remarked, and started at the death-like image of the youth; "look not thus, or you will utterly unman me."

A sudden and involuntary impulse caused him to extend his arms. The young officer sprang forward into the proffered embrace, and sank his head upon the cheek of his father. It was the first time he had enjoyed that privilege since his childhood; and even overwhelmed as he was by his affliction, he felt it deeply.

This short but touching scene was witnessed by their companions, without levity in any, and with emotion by several. None felt more gratified at this demonstration of parental affection for the sensitive boy, than Blessington and Erskine.

"I cannot yet persuade myself," observed the former officer, as the colonel again assumed that dignity of demeanour which had been momentarily lost sight of in the ebullition of his feelings,—"I cannot yet persuade myself things are altogether so bad as they appear. It is true the schooner is in the possession of the enemy, but there is nothing to prove our friends are on board."

"If you had reason to know HIM into whose hands she has fallen, as I do, you would think differently, Captain Blessington," returned the governor. "That mysterious being," he pursued, after a short pause, "would never have made this parade of his conquest, had it related merely to a few lives, which to him are of utter insignificance. The very substitution of yon black flag, in his insolent triumph, was the pledge of redemption of a threat breathed in my ear within this very fort: on what occasion I need not state, since the events connected with that unhappy night are still fresh in the recollections of us all. That he is my personal enemy, gentlemen, it would be vain to disguise from you; although who he is, or of what nature his enmity, it imports not now to enter upon Suffice it, I have little doubt my children are in his power; but whether the black flag indicates they are no more, or that the tragedy is only in preparation, I confess I am at a loss to understand."

Deeply affected by the evident despondency that had dictated these unusual admissions on the part of their chief, the officers were forward to combat the inferences he had drawn: several coinciding in the opinion now expressed by Captain Wentworth, that the fact of the schooner having fallen into the hands of the savages by no means implied the capture of the fort whence she came; since it was not at all unlikely she had been chased during a calm by the numerous canoes into the Sinclair, where, owing to the extreme narrowness of the river, she had fallen an easy prey.

"Moreover," observed Captain Blessington, "it is highly improbable the ferocious warrior could have succeeded in capturing any others than the unfortunate crew of the schooner; for had this been the case, he would not have lost the opportunity of crowning his triumph by exhibiting his victims to our view in some conspicuous part of the vessel."

"This, I grant you," rejoined the governor, "to be one solitary circumstance in our favour; but may it not, after all, merely prove that our worst apprehensions are already realised?"

"He is not one, methinks, since vengeance seems his aim, to exercise it in so summary, and therefore merciful, a manner. Depend upon it, colonel, had any of those in whom we are more immediately interested, fallen into his hands, he would not have failed to insult and agonize us by an exhibition of his prisoners."

"You are right, Blessington," exclaimed Charles de Haldimar, in a voice that his choking feelings rendered almost sepulchral; "he is not one to exercise his vengeance in a summary, and merciful manner. The deed is yet unaccomplished, for even now the curse of Ellen Halloway

95

rings again in my ear, and tells me the atoning blood must be spilt on the grave of her husband."

The peculiar tone in which these words were uttered, caused every one present to turn and regard the speaker, for they recalled the prophetic language of the unhappy woman. There was now a wildness of expression in his handsome features, marking the mind utterly dead to hope, yet struggling to work itself up to passive endurance of the worst. Colonel de Haldimar sighed painfully, as he bent his eye half reproachfully on the dull and attenuated features of his son; and although he spoke not, his look betrayed the anguish that allusion had called up to his heart.

"Forgive me, my father," exclaimed the youth, grasping a hand that was reluctantly extended. "I meant it not in unkindness; but indeed I have ever had the conviction strongly impressed on my spirit. I know I appear weak, childish, unsoldierlike; yet can it be wondered at, when I have been so often latterly deceived by false hopes, that now my heart has room for no other tenant than despair. I am very wretched," he pursued, with affecting despondency; "in the presence of my companions do I admit it, but they all know how I loved my sister. Can they then feel surprise, that having lost not only her, but my brother and my friend, I should be the miserable thing I am."

Colonel de Haldimar turned away, much affected; and throwing his back against the sentry box near him, passed his hand over his eyes, and remained for a few moments motionless.

"Charles, Charles, is this your promise to me?" whispered Captain Blessington, as he approached and took the hand of his unhappy friend. "Is this the self-command you pledged yourself to exercise? For Heaven's sake, agitate not your father thus, by the indulgence of a grief that can have no other tendency than to render him equally wretched. Be advised by me, and quit the rampart. Return to your guard, and endeavour to compose yourself."

"Ha! what new movement is that on the part of the savages?" exclaimed Captain Erskine, who had kept his glass to his eye mechanically, and chiefly with a view of hiding the emotion produced in him by the almost infantine despair of the younger De Haldimar: "surely it is—yet, no, it cannot be—yes, see how they are dragging several prisoners from the wood to the beach. I can distinctly see a man in a blanket coat, and two others considerably taller, and apparently sailors. But look, behind them are two females in European dress. Almighty Heaven! there can be no doubt."

A painful pause ensued. Every other glass and eye was levelled in the same direction; and, even as Erskine had described it, a party of Indians were seen, by those who had the telescopes, conducting five prisoners towards a canoe that lay in the channel communicating from the island with the main land on the Detroit shore. Into the bottom of these they were presently huddled, so that only their heads and shoulders were visible above the gunwale of the frail bark. Presently a tall warrior was seen bounding from the wood towards the beach. The crowd of gesticulating Indians made way, and the warrior was seen to stoop and apply his shoulder to the canoe, one half of which was high and dry upon the sands. The heavily laden vessel obeyed the impetus with a rapidity that proved the muscular power of him who gave it. Like some wild animal, instinct with life, it lashed the foaming waters from its bows, and left a deep and gurgling furrow where it passed. As it quitted the shore, the warrior sprang lightly in, taking his station at the stern; and while his tall and remarkable figure bent nimbly to the movement, he dashed his paddle from right to left alternately in the stream, with a quickness that rendered it almost invisible to the eye. Presently the canoe disappeared round an intervening headland, and the officers lost sight of it altogether.

"The portrait, Charles; what have you done with the portrait?" exclaimed Captain Blessington, actuated by a sudden recollection, and with a trepidation in his voice and manner that spoke volumes of despair to the younger De Haldimar. "This is our only hope of solving the mystery. Quick, give me the portrait, if you have it."

The young officer hurriedly tore the miniature from the breast of his uniform, and pitched it through the interval that separated him from his captain, who stood a few feet off; but with so uncertain and trembling an aim, it missed the hand extended to secure it, and fell upon the very stone the youth had formerly pointed out to Blessington, as marking the particular spot on which he stood during the execution of Halloway. The violence of the fall separated the back of the frame from the picture itself, when suddenly a piece of white and crumpled paper, apparently part of the back of a letter, yet cut to the size and shape of the miniature, was exhibited to the view of all.

"Ha!" resumed the gratified Blessington, as he stooped to possess himself of the prize; "I knew the miniature would be found to contain some intelligence from our friends. It is only this moment it occurred to me to take it to pieces, but accident has anticipated my purpose. May the omen prove a good one! But what have we here?"

With some difficulty, the anxious officer now succeeded in making out the characters, which, in default of pen or pencil, had been formed by the pricking of a fine pin on the paper. The broken sentences, on which the whole of the group now hung with greedy ear, ran nearly as follows:—"All is lost. Michilimackinac is taken. We are prisoners, and doomed to die within eight and forty hours. Alas! Clara and Madeline are of our number. Still there is a hope, if my father deem it prudent to incur the risk. A surprise, well managed, may do much; but it must be tomorrow night; forty-eight hours more, and it will be of no avail. He who will deliver this is our friend, and the enemy of my father's enemy. He will be in the same spot at the same hour to-morrow night, and will conduct the detachment to wherever we may chance to be. If you fail in your enterprise, receive our last prayers for a less disastrous fate. God bless you all!"

The blood ran coldly through every vein during the perusal of these important sentences, but not one word of comment was offered by an individual of the group. No explanation was necessary. The captives in the canoe, the tall warrior in its stern, all sufficiently betrayed the horrible truth.

Colonel de Haldimar at length turned an enquiring look at his two captains, and then addressing the adjutant, asked—

"What companies are off duty to-day, Mr. Lawson?"

"Mine," said Blessington, with an energy that denoted how deeply rejoiced he felt at the fact, and without giving the adjutant time to reply.

"And mine," impetuously added Captain Erskine; "and, by G—! I will answer for them; they never embarked on a duty of the sort with greater zeal than they will on this occasion."

"Gentlemen, I thank you," said Colonel de Haldimar, with deep emotion, as he stepped forward and grasped in turn the hands of the generous-hearted officers. "To Heaven, and to your exertions, do I commit my children."

"Any artillery, colonel?" enquired the officer of that corps.

"No, Wentworth, no artillery. Whatever remains to be done, must be achieved by the bayonet alone, and under favour of the darkness. Gentlemen, again I thank you for this generous interest in my children—this forwardness in an enterprise on which depend the lives of so many dear friends. I am not one given to express warm emotion, but I do, indeed, appreciate this conduct deeply." He then moved away, desiring Mr. Lawson, as he quitted the rampart, to cause the men for this service to be got in instant readiness.

Following the example of their colonel, Captains Blessington and Erskine quitted the rampart also, hastening to satisfy themselves by personal inspection of the efficiency in all respects of their several companies; and in a few minutes, the only individual to be seen in that quarter of the works was the sentinel, who had been a silent and pained witness of all that had passed among his officers.

CHAPTER VI.

Doubtless, many of our readers are prepared to expect that the doom of the unfortunate Frank Halloway was, as an officer of his regiment had already hinted, the fruit of some personal pique and concealed motive of vengeance; and that the denouement of our melancholy story will afford evidence of the governor's knowledge of the true character of him, who, under an assumed name, excited such general interest at his trial and death, not only among his military superiors, but those with whom his adverse destiny had more immediately associated him. It has already been urged to us, by one or two of our critical friends to whom we have submitted what has been thus far written in our tale, that, to explain satisfactorily and consistently the extreme severity of the governor, some secret and personally influencing motive must be assigned; but to these we have intimated, what we now repeat,—namely, that we hope to bear out our story, by natural explanation and simple deduction. Who Frank Halloway really was, or what the connection existing between him and the mysterious enemy of the family of De Haldimar, the sequel of our narrative will show; but whatever its nature, and however well founded the apprehension of the governor of the formidable being hitherto known as the warrior of the Fleur de lis, and however strong his conviction that the devoted Halloway and his enemy were in secret correspondence, certain it is, that, to the very hour of the death of the former, he knew him as no other than the simple private soldier.

To have ascribed to Colonel de Haldimar motives that would have induced his eagerly seeking the condemnation of an innocent man, either to gratify a thirst of vengeance, or to secure immunity against personal danger, would have been to have painted him, not only as a villain, but a coward. Colonel de Haldimar was neither; but, on the contrary, what is understood in worldly parlance and the generally received acceptation of the terms, a man of strict integrity and honour, as well as of the most undisputed courage. Still, he was a severe and a haughty man,—one whose military education had been based on the principles of the old school—and to whom the command of a regiment afforded a field for the exercise of an orthodox despotism, that could not be passed over without the immolation of many a victim on its rugged surface. Without ever having possessed any thing like acute feeling, his heart, as nature had formed it, was moulded to receive the ordinary impressions of humanity; and had he been doomed to move in the sphere of private life, if he had not been distinguished by any remarkable sensibilities, he would not, in all probability, have been conspicuous for any extraordinary cruelties. Sent into the army, however, at an early age, and with a blood not remarkable for its mercurial aptitudes, he had calmly and deliberately imbibed all the starched theories and standard prejudices which a mind by no means naturally gifted was but too well predisposed to receive; and he was among the number of those (many of whom are indigenous to our soil even at the present day) who look down from a rank obtained, upon that which has been just quitted, with a contempt, and coldness, and consciousness of elevation, commensurate only with the respect paid to those still above them, and which it belongs only to the little-minded to indulge in.

As a subaltern, M. de Haldimar had ever been considered a pattern of rigid propriety and decorum of conduct. Not the shadow of military crime had ever been laid to his charge. He was punctual at all parades and drills; kept the company to which he was attached in a perfect hot water of discipline; never missed his distance in marching past, or failed in a military manoeuvre; paid his mess-bill regularly to the hour, nay, minute, of the settling day; and was never, on any one occasion, known to enter the paymaster's office, except on the well-remembered 24th of each month; and, to crown all, he had never asked, consequently never obtained, a day's leave from his regiment, although he had served in it so long, that there was now but one man living who had entered it with him. With all these qualities, Ensign de Haldimar promised to make an excellent soldier; and, as such, was encouraged by the field-officers of the corps, who unhesitatingly pronounced him a lad of discernment and talent, who would one day rival them in all the glorious privileges of martinetism. It was even remarked, as an evidence of his worth, that, when promoted to a lieutenancy, he looked down upon the ensigns with that becoming condescension which befitted his new rank; and up to the captains with the deferential respect he felt to be due to that third step in the five-barred gate of regimental promotion, on which his aspiring but chained foot had not yet succeeded in reposing. What, therefore, he became when he had succeeded in clambering to the top, and looked down from the lordly height he had after many years of plodding service obtained, we must leave it to the imaginations of our readers to determine. We reserve it to a future page, to relate more interesting particulars.

Sufficient has been shown, however, from this outline of his character, as well as from the conversations among his officers, elsewhere transcribed, to account for the governor's conduct in the case of Halloway. That the recommendation of his son, Captain de Haldimar, had not been attended to, arose not from any particular ill-will towards the unhappy man, but simply because he had always been in the habit of making his own selections from the ranks, and that the present recommendation had been warmly urged by one who he fancied pretended to a discrimination superior to his own, in pointing out merits that had escaped his observation. It might be, too, that there was a latent pride about the manner of Halloway that displeased and dissatisfied one who looked upon his subordinates as things that were amenable to the haughtiness of his glance,—not enough of deference in his demeanour, or of supplicating obsequiousness in his speech, to entitle him to the promotion prayed for. Whatever the motive, there was nothing of personality to influence him in the rejection of the appeal made in favour of one who had never injured him; but who, on the contrary, as the whole of the regiment could attest, had saved the life of his son.

Rigid disciplinarian as he was, and holding himself responsible for the safety of the garrison it was but natural, when the discovery had been made of the unaccountable unfastening of the gate of the fort, suspicion of no ordinary kind should attach to the sentinel posted there; and that he should steadily refuse all credence to a story wearing so much appearance of improbability. Proud, and inflexible, and bigoted to first impressions, his mind was closed against those palliating circumstances, which, adduced by Halloway in his defence, had so mainly contributed to stamp the conviction of his moral innocence on the minds of his judges and the attentive auditory; and could he even have conquered his pride so far as to have admitted the belief of that innocence, still the military crime of which he had been guilty, in infringing a positive order of the garrison, was in itself sufficient to call forth all the unrelenting severity of his nature. Throughout the whole of the proceedings subsequently instituted, he had acted and spoken from a perfect conviction of the treason of the unfortunate soldier, and with the fullest impression of the falsehood of all that had been offered in his defence. The considerations that influenced the minds of his officers, found no entrance into his proud breast, which was closed against every thing but his own dignified sense of superior judgment. Could he, like them, have given credence to the tale of Halloway, or really have believed that Captain de Haldimar, educated under his own military eye, could have been so wanting in subordination, as not merely to have infringed a positive order of the garrison, but to have made a private soldier of that garrison accessary to his delinquency, it is more than probable his stern habits of military discipline would have caused him to overlook the offence of the soldier, in deeper indignation at the conduct of the infinitely more culpable officer; but not one word did he credit of a statement, which he assumed to have been got up by the prisoner with the mere view of shielding himself from punishment: and when to these suspicions of his fidelity was attached the fact of the introduction of his alarming visitor, it must be confessed his motives for indulging in this belief were not without foundation.

The impatience manifested during the trial of Halloway was not a result of any desire of systematic persecution, but of a sense of wounded dignity. It was a thing unheard of, and unpardonable in his eyes, for a private soldier to assert, in his presence, his honour and his respectability in extenuation, even while admitting the justice of a specific charge; and when he remarked the Court listening with that profound attention, which the peculiar history of the prisoner had excited, he could not repress the manifestation of his anger. In justice to him, however, it must be acknowledged that, in causing the charge, to which the unfortunate man pleaded guilty, to be framed, he had only acted from the conviction that, on the two first, there was not sufficient evidence to condemn one whose crime was as clearly established, to his judgment, as if he had been an eye-witness of the treason. It is true, he availed himself of Halloway's voluntary confession, to effect his condemnation; but estimating him as a traitor, he felt little delicacy was necessary to be observed on that score.

Much of the despotic military character of Colonel de Haldimar had been communicated to his private life; so much, indeed, that his sons,—both of whom, it has been seen, were of natures that belied their origin from so stern a stock,—were kept at nearly as great a distance from him as any other subordinates of his regiment. But although he seldom indulged in manifestations of parental regard towards those whom he looked upon rather as inferiors in military rank, than as beings connected with him by the ties of blood, Colonel de Haldimar was not without that instinctive love for his children, which every animal in the creation feels for its offspring. He, also, valued and took a pride in, because they reflected a certain degree of lustre upon himself, the talents and accomplishments of his eldest son, who, moreover, was a brave, enterprising officer, and, only wanted, in his father's estimation, that severity of carriage and hauteur of deportment, befitting HIS son, to render him perfect. As for Charles,—the gentle, bland, winning, universally conciliating Charles,—he looked upon him as a mere weak boy, who could never hope to arrive at any post of distinction, if only by reason of the extreme delicacy of his physical organisation; and to have shown any thing like respect for his character, or indulged in any expression of tenderness for one so far below his estimate of what a soldier, a child of his, ought to be, would have been a concession of which his proud nature was incapable. In his daughter Clara, however, the gentleness of sex claimed that warmer affection which was denied to him, who resembled her in almost every attribute of mind and person. Colonel de Haldimar doated on his daughter with a tenderness, for which few, who were familiar with his harsh and unbending nature, ever gave him credit. She was the image of one on whom all of love that he had ever known had been centered;

and he had continued in Clara an affection, that seemed in itself to form a portion, distinct and apart, of his existence.

We have already seen, as stated by Charles de Haldimar to the unfortunate wife of Halloway, with what little success he had pleaded in the interview he had requested of his father, for the preserver of his gallant brother's life; and we have also seen how equally inefficient was the lowly and supplicating anguish of that wretched being, when, on quitting the apartment of his son, Colonel de Haldimar had so unexpectedly found himself clasped in her despairing embrace. There was little to be expected from an intercession on the part of one claiming so little ascendancy over his father's heart, as the universally esteemed young officer; still less from one who, in her shriek of agony, had exposed the haughty chief to the observation both of men and officers, and under circumstances that caused his position to border on the ludicrous. But however these considerations might have failed in effect, there was another which, as a soldier, he could not wholly overlook. Although he had offered no comment on the extraordinary recommendation to mercy annexed to the sentence of the prisoner, it had had a certain weight with him; and he felt, all absolute even as he was, he could not, without exciting strong dissatisfaction among his troops, refuse attention to a document so powerfully worded, and bearing the signature and approval of so old and valued an officer as Captain

Blessington. His determination, therefore, had been formed, even before his visit to his son, to act as circumstances might require; and, in the mean while, he commanded every preparation for the execution to be made.

In causing a strong detachment to be marched to the conspicuous point chosen for his purpose, he had acted from a conviction of the necessity of showing the enemy the treason of the soldier had been detected; reserving to himself the determination of carrying the sentence into full effect, or pardoning the condemned, as the event might warrant. Not one moment, meanwhile, did he doubt the guilt of Halloway, whose description of the person of his enemy was, in itself, to him, confirmatory evidence of his treason. It is doubtful whether he would, in any way, have been influenced by the recommendation of the Court, had the first charges been substantiated; but as there was nothing but conjecture to bear out these, and as the prisoner had been convicted only on the ground of suffering Captain de Haldimar to quit the fort contrary to orders, he felt he might possibly go too far in carrying the capital punishment into effect, in decided opposition to the general feeling of the garrison,—both of officers and men.

When the shot was subsequently fired from the hut of the Canadian, and the daring rifleman recognised as the same fearful individual who had gained access to his apartment the preceding night, conviction of the guilt of Halloway came

111

even deeper home to the mind of the governor. It was through Francois alone that a communication was kept up secretly between the garrison and several of the Canadians without the fort; and the very fact of the mysterious warrior having been there so recently after his daring enterprise, bore evidence that whatever treason was in operation, had been carried on through the instrumentality of mine host of the Fleur de lis. In proof, moreover, there was the hat of Donellan, and the very rope Halloway had stated to be that by which the unfortunate officer had effected his exit. Colonel de Haldimar was not one given to indulge in the mysterious or to believe in the romantic. Every thing was plain matter of fact, as it now appeared before him; and he thought it evident, as though it had been written in words of fire, that if his son and his unfortunate servant had quitted the fort in the manner represented, it was no less certain they had been forced off by a party, at the head of whom was his vindictive enemy, and with the connivance of Halloway. We have seen, that after the discovery of the sex of the supposed drummer-boy when the prisoners were confronted together, Colonel de Haldimar had closely watched the expression of their countenances, but failed in discovering any thing that could be traced into evidence of a guilty recognition. Still he conceived his original impression to have been too forcibly borne out, even by the events of the last half hour, to allow this to have much weight with him; and his determination to carry the thing through all its fearful preliminary stages became more and more confirmed.

In adopting this resolution in the first instance, he was not without a hope that Halloway, standing, as he must feel himself to be, on the verge of the grave, might be induced to make confession of his guilt, and communicate whatever particulars might prove essential not only to the safety of the garrison generally, but to himself individually, as far as his personal enemy was concerned. With this view, he had charged Captain Blessington, in the course of their march from the hut to the fatal bridge, to promise a full pardon, provided he should make such confession of his crime as would lead to a just appreciation of the evils likely to result from the treason that had in part been accomplished. Even in making this provision, however, which was met by the prisoner with solemn yet dignified reiteration of his innocence, Colonel de Haldimar had not made the refusal of pardon altogether conclusive in his own mind: still, in adopting this plan, there was a chance of obtaining a confession; and not until there was no longer a prospect of the unhappy man being led into that confession, did he feel it imperative on him to stay the progress of the tragedy.

What the result would have been, had not Halloway, in the strong excitement of his feelings, sprung to his feet upon the coffin, uttering the exclamation of triumph recorded in the last pages of our first volume, is scarcely doubtful. However much the governor might have contemned and slighted a credulity in which he in no way participated himself, he had too much discrimination not to perceive, that to have persevered in the capital punishment would have been to have rendered himself personally obnoxious to the comrades of the condemned, whose dispirited air and sullen mien, he clearly saw, denounced the punishment as one of unnecessary rigour. The haughty commander was not one to be intimidated by manifestations of discontent; neither was he one to brook a spirit of insubordination, however forcibly supported; but he had too much experience and military judgment, not to determine that this was riot a moment, by foregoing an act of compulsory clemency, to instil divisions in the garrison, when the safety of all so much depended on the cheerfulness and unanimity with which they lent themselves to the arduous duties of defence.

However originating in policy, the lenity he might have been induced to have shown, all idea of the kind was chased from his mind by the unfortunate action of the prisoner. At the moment when the distant heights resounded with the fierce yells of the savages, and leaping forms came bounding down the slope, the remarkable warrior of the Fleur de lis— the fearful enemy who had whispered the most demoniac vengeance in his ears the preceding night—was the only one that met and riveted the gaze of the governor. He paused not to observe or to think who the flying man could be of whom the mysterious warrior was in pursuit,—neither did it, indeed, occur to him that it was a pursuit at all. But one idea suggested itself to his mind, and that was an attempt at rescue of the condemned on the part of his accomplice; and when at length Halloway, who had at once, as if by instinct, recognised his captain in the fugitive, shouted forth his gratitude to Heaven that "he at length approached who alone had the power to save him," every shadow of mercy was banished from the mind of the governor, who, labouring under a natural misconception of the causes of his exulting shout, felt that justice imperatively demanded her victim, and no longer hesitated in awarding the doom that became the supposed traitor. It was under this impression that he sternly gave and repeated the fatal order to fire; and by this misjudged and severe, although not absolutely cruel act, not only destroyed one of the noblest beings that ever wore a soldier's uniform, but entailed upon himself and family that terrific curse of his maniac wife, which rang like a prophetic warning in the ears of all, and was often heard in the fitful starlings of his own ever-after troubled slumbers.

What his feelings were, when subsequently he discovered, in the wretched fugitive, the son whom he already believed to have been numbered with the dead, and heard from his lips a confirmation of all that had been advanced by the unhappy Halloway, we shall leave it to our readers to imagine. Still, even amid his first regret, the rigid disciplinarian was strong within him; and no sooner had the detachment regained the fort, after performing the last offices of interment over their ill-fated comrade, than Captain de Haldimar received an intimation, through the adjutant, to consider himself under close arrest for disobedience of orders. Finally, however, he succeeded in procuring an interview with his father; in the course of which, disclosing the plot of the Indians, and the short period allotted for its being carried into execution, he painted in the most gloomy colours the alarming, dangers which threatened them all, and finished by urgently imploring his father to suffer him to make the attempt to reach their unsuspecting friends at Michilimackinac. Fully impressed with the difficulties attendant on a scheme that offered so few feasible chances of success, Colonel de Haldimar for a period denied his concurrence; but when at length the excited young man dwelt on the horrors that would inevitably await his sister and betrothed cousin, were they to fall into the hands of the savages, these considerations were found to be effective. An after-arrangement included Sir Everard Valletort, who had expressed a strong desire to share his danger in the enterprise; and the services of the Canadian, who had been brought back a prisoner to the fort, and on whom promises and threats were bestowed in an equally lavish manner, were rendered available. In fact, without the assistance of Francois, there was little chance of their effecting in safety the navigation of the waters through which they were to pass to arrive at the fort. He it was, who, when summoned to attend a conference among the officers, bearing on the means to be adopted, suggested the propriety of their disguising themselves as Canadian duck hunters; in which character they might expect to pass unmolested, even if encountered by any outlying parties of the savages. With the doubts that had previously been entertained of the fidelity of Francois, there was an air of forlorn hope given to the enterprise; still, as the man expressed sincere earnestness of desire to repay the clemency accorded him, by a faithful exercise of his services, and as the object sought was one that justified the risk, there was, notwithstanding, a latent hope cherished by all parties, that the event would prove successful. We have already seen to what extent their anticipations were realised.

Whether it was that he secretly acknowledged the too excessive sternness of his justice in regard to Halloway (who still, in the true acceptation of facts, had been guilty of a crime that entailed the penalty he had paid), or that the apprehensions that arose to his heart in regard to her on whom he yearned with all a father's fondness governed his conduct, certain it is, that, from the hour of the disclosure made by his son, Colonel de Haldimar became an altered man. Without losing any thing of that dignity of manner, which had hitherto been confounded with the most repellent haughtiness of bearing, his demeanour towards his officers became more courteous; and although, as heretofore, he kept himself entirely aloof, except when occasions of duty brought them together, still, when they did meet, there was more of conciliation in his manner, and less of austerity in his speech. There was, moreover, a dejection in his eye, strongly in contrast with his former imperious glance; and more than one officer remarked, that, if his days were devoted to the customary practical arrangements for defence, his pallid countenance betokened that his nights were nights rather of vigil than of repose.

However natural and deep the alarm entertained for the fate of the sister fort, there could be no apprehension on the mind of Colonel de Haldimar in regard to his own; since, furnished with the means of foiling his enemies with their own weapons of cunning and deceit, a few extraordinary precautions alone were necessary to secure all immunity from danger. Whatever might be the stern peculiarities of his character,—and these had originated chiefly in an education purely military,—Colonel de Haldimar was an officer well calculated to the important trust reposed in him; for, combining experience with judgment in all matters relating to the diplomacy of war, and being fully conversant with the character and habits of the enemy opposed to him, he possessed singular aptitude to seize whatever advantages might present themselves.

The prudence and caution of his policy have already been made manifest in the two several council scenes with the chiefs recorded in our second volume. It may appear singular, that, with the opportunity thus afforded him of retaining the formidable Ponteac,—the strength and sinew of that long protracted and ferocious war,—in his power, he should have waved his advantage; but here Colonel de Haldimar gave evidence of the tact which so eminently distinguished his public conduct throughout. He well knew the noble, fearless character of the chief; and felt, if any hold was to be secured over him, it was by grappling with his generosity, and not by the exercise of intimidation. Even admitting that Ponteac continued his prisoner, and that the troops, pouring their destructive fire upon the mass of enemies so suddenly arrested on the drawbridge, had swept away the whole, still they were but as a mite among the numerous nations that were leagued against the English; and to these nations, it was evident, they must, sooner or later, succumb.

Colonel de Haldimar knew enough of the proud but generous nature of the Ottawa, to deem that the policy he proposed to pursue in the last council scene would not prove altogether without effect on that warrior. It was well known to him, that much pains had been taken to instil into the minds of the Indians the belief that the English were resolved on their final extirpation; and as certain slights, offered to them at various periods, had given a colouring of truth to this assertion, the formidable league which had already accomplished the downfall of so many of the forts had been the consequence of these artful representations. Although well aware that the French had numerous emissaries distributed among the fierce tribes, it was not until after the disclosure made by the haughty Ponteac, at the close of the first council scene, that he became apprised of the alarming influence exercised over the mind of that warrior himself by his own terrible and vindictive enemy. The necessity of counteracting that influence was obvious; and he felt this was only to be done (if at all) by some marked and extraordinary evidence of the peaceful disposition of the English. Hence his determination to suffer the faithless chiefs and their followers to depart unharmed from the fort, even at the moment when the attitude assumed by the prepared garrison fully proved to the assailants their designs had been penetrated and their schemes rendered abortive.

CHAPTER VII.

With the general position of the encampment of the investing Indians, the reader has been made acquainted through the narrative of Captain de Haldimar. It was, as has been shown, situate in a sort of oasis close within the verge of the forest, and (girt by an intervening underwood which Nature, in her caprice, had fashioned after the manner of a defensive barrier) embraced a space sufficient to contain the tents of the fighting men, together with their women and children. This, however, included only the warriors and inferior chiefs. The tents of the leaders were without the belt of underwood, and principally distributed at long intervals on that side of the forest which skirted the open country towards the river; forming, as it were, a chain of external defences, and sweeping in a semicircular direction round the more dense encampment of their followers. At its highest elevation the forest shot out suddenly into a point, naturally enough rendered an object of attraction from whatever part it was commanded.

Darkness was already beginning to spread her mantle over the intervening space, and the night fires of the Indians were kindling into brightness, glimmering occasionally through the wood with that pale and lambent light peculiar to the fire-fly, of which they offered a not inapt representation, when suddenly a lofty tent, the brilliant whiteness of which was thrown into strong relief by the dark field on which it reposed, was seen to rise at a few paces from the abrupt point in the forest just described, and on the extreme summit of a ridge, beyond which lay only the western horizon in golden perspective.

The opening of this tent looked eastward and towards the fort; and on its extreme summit floated a dark flag, which at intervals spread itself before the slight evening breeze, but oftener hung drooping and heavily over the glittering canvass. One solitary pine, whose trunk exceeded not the ordinary thickness of a man's waist, and standing out as a landmark on the ridge, rose at the distance of a few feet from the spot on which the tent had been erected; and to this was bound the tall and elegant figure of one dressed in the coarse garb of a sailor. The arms and legs of this individual were perfectly free; but a strong rope, rendered doubly secure after the manner of what is termed "whipping" among seamen, after having been tightly drawn several times around his waist, and then firmly knotted behind, was again passed round the tree, to which the back of the prisoner was closely lashed; thus enabling, or rather compelling, him to be a spectator of every object within the tent.

Layers of bark, over which were spread the dressed skins of the bear and the buffalo, formed the floor and carpet of the latter; and on these, in various parts, and in characteristic attitudes, reposed the forms of three human beings;—one, the formidable warrior of the Fleur de lis. Attired in the garb in which we first introduced him to our readers, and with the same weapons reposing at his side, the haughty savage lay at his lazy length; his feet reaching beyond the opening of the tent, and his head reposing on a rude pillow formed of a closely compressed pack of skins of wild animals, over which was spread a sort of mantle or blanket. One hand was introduced between the pillow and his head, the other grasped the pipe tomahawk he was smoking; and while the mechanical play of his right foot indicated pre-occupation of thought, his quick and meaning eye glanced frequently and alternately upon the furthest of his companions, the prisoner without, and the distant fort.

Within a few feet of the warrior lay, extended on a buffalo skin, the delicate figure of a female, whose hair, complexion, and hands, denoted her European extraction. Her dress was entirely Indian, however; consisting of a machecoti with leggings, mocassins, and shirt of printed cotton studded with silver brooches,—all of which were of a quality and texture to mark the wearer as the wife of a chief; and her fair hair, done up in a club behind, reposed on a neck of dazzling whiteness. Her eyes were large, blue, but wild and unmeaning; her countenance vacant; and her movements altogether mechanical. A wooden bowl filled with hominy,— a preparation of Indian corn,—was at her side; and from this she was now in the act of feeding herself with a spoon of the same material, but with a negligence and slovenliness that betrayed her almost utter unconsciousness of the action.

At the further side of the tent there was another woman, even more delicate in appearance than the one last mentioned. She, too, was blue-eyed, and of surpassing fairness of skin. Her attitude denoted a mind too powerfully absorbed in grief to be heedful of appearances; for she sat with her knees drawn up to her chin, and rocking her body to and fro with an undulating motion that seemed to have its origin in no effort of volition of her own. Her long fair hair hung negligently over her shoulders; and a blanket drawn over the top of her head like a veil, and extending partly over the person, disclosed here and there portions of an apparel which was strictly European, although rent, and exhibiting in various places stains of blood. A bowl similar to that of her companion, and filled with the same food, was at her side; but this was untasted.

"Why does the girl refuse to eat?" asked the warrior of her next him, as he fiercely rolled a volume of smoke from his lips. "Make her eat, for I would speak to her afterwards."

"Why does the girl refuse to eat?" responded the woman in the same tone, dropping her spoon as she spoke, and turning to the object of remark with a vacant look. "It is good," she pursued, as she rudely shook the arm of the heedless sufferer. "Come, girl, eat."

A shriek burst from the lips of the unhappy girl, as, apparently roused from her abstraction, she suffered the blanket to fall from her head, and staring wildly at her questioner, faintly demanded,—

"Who, in the name of mercy, are you, who address me in this horrid place in my own tongue? Speak; who are you? Surely I should know that voice for that of Ellen, the wife of Frank Halloway!"

A maniac laugh was uttered by the wretched woman. This continued offensively for a moment; and she observed, in an infuriated tone and with a searching eye,—"No, I am not the wife of Halloway. It is false. I am the wife of Wacousta. This is my husband!" and as she spoke she sprang nimbly to her feet, and was in the next instant lying prostrate on the form of the warrior; her arms thrown wildly around him, and her lips imprinting kisses on his cheek.

But Wacousta was in no mood to suffer her endearments. He for the first time seemed alive to the presence of her who lay beyond, and, to whose whole appearance a character of animation had been imparted by the temporary excitement of her feelings. He gazed at her a moment, with the air of one endeavouring to recall the memory of days long gone by; and as he continued to do so, his eye dilated, his chest heaved, and his countenance alternately flushed and paled. At length he threw the form that reposed upon his own, violently, and even savagely, from him; sprang eagerly to his feet; and clearing the space that divided him from the object of his attention at a single step, bore her from the earth in his arms with as much ease as if she had been an infant, and then returning to his own rude couch, placed his horror-stricken victim at his side.

"Nay, nay," he urged sarcastically, as she vainly struggled to free herself; "let the De Haldimar portion of your blood rise up in anger if it will; but that of Clara Beverley, at least—."

"Gracious Providence! where am I, that I hear the name of my sainted mother thus familiarly pronounced?" interrupted the startled girl; "and who are you,"—turning her eyes wildly on the swarthy countenance of the warrior,—"who are you, I ask, who, with the mien and in the garb of a savage of these forests, appear thus acquainted with her name?"

The warrior passed his hand across his brow for a moment, as if some painful and intolerable reflection had been called up by the question; but he speedily recovered his self-possession, and, with an expression of feature that almost petrified his auditor, vehemently observed,—

"You ask who I am! One who knew your mother long before the accursed name of De Haldimar had even been whispered in her ear; and whom love for the one and hatred for the other has rendered the savage you now behold! But," he continued, while a fierce and hideous smile lighted up every feature, "I overlook my past sufferings in my present happiness. The image of Clara Beverley, even such as my soul loved her in its youth, is once more before me in her child; THAT child shall be my wife!"

"Your wife! monster;—never!" shrieked the unhappy girl, again vainly attempting to disengage herself from the encircling arm of the savage. "But," she pursued, in a tone of supplication, while the tears coursed each other down her cheek, "if you ever loved my mother as you say you have, restore her children to their home; and, if saints may be permitted to look down from heaven in approval of the acts of men, she whom you have loved will bless you for the deed."

A deep groan burst from the vast chest of Wacousta; but, for a moment, he answered not. At length he observed, pointing at the same time with his finger towards the cloudless vault above their heads,—"Do you behold yon blue sky, Clara de Haldimar?"

"I do;—what mean you?" demanded the trembling girl, in whom a momentary hope had been excited by the subdued manner of the savage.

"Nothing," he coolly rejoined; "only that were your mother to appear there at this moment, clad in all the attributes ascribed to angels, her prayer would not alter the destiny that awaits you. Nay, nay; look not thus sorrowfully," he pursued, as, in despite of her efforts to prevent him, he imprinted a burning kiss upon her lips. "Even thus was I once wont to linger on the lips of your mother; but hers ever pouted to be pressed by mine; and not with tears, but with sunniest smiles, did she court them." He paused; bent his head over the face of the shuddering girl; and gazing fixedly for a few minutes on her countenance, while he pressed her struggling form more closely to his own, exultingly pursued, as if to himself,—"Even as her mother was, so is she. Ye powers of hell! who would have ever thought a time would come when both my vengeance and my love would be gratified to the utmost? How strange it never should have occurred to me he had a daughter!"

"What mean you, fierce, unpitying man?" exclaimed the terrified Clara, to whom a full sense of the horror of her position had lent unusual energy of character. "Surely you will not detain a poor defenceless woman in your hands,— the child of her you say you have loved. But it is false!—you never knew her, or you would not now reject my prayer."

"Never knew her!" fiercely repeated Wacousta. Again he paused. "Would I had never known her! and I should not now be the outcast wretch I am," he added, slowly and impressively. Then once more elevating his voice,—"Clara de Haldimar, I have loved your mother as man never loved woman; and I have hated your father" (grinding his teeth with fury as he spoke) "as man never hated man. That love, that hatred are unquenched—unquenchable. Before me I see at once the image of her who, even in death, has lived enshrined in my heart, and the child of him who is my bitterest foe. Clara de Haldimar, do you understand me now?"

"Almighty Providence! is there no one to save me?—can nothing touch your stubborn heart?" exclaimed the affrighted girl; and she turned her swimming eyes on those of the warrior, in appeal; but his glance caused her own to sink in confusion. "Ellen Halloway," she pursued, after a moment's pause, and in the wild accents of despair, "if you are indeed the wife of this man, as you say you are, oh! plead for me with him; and in the name of that kindness, which I once extended to yourself, prevail on him to restore me to my father!"

"Ellen Halloway!—who calls Ellen Halloway?" said the wretched woman, who had again resumed her slovenly meal on the rude couch, apparently without consciousness of the scene enacting at her side. "I am not Ellen Halloway: they said so; but it is not true. My husband was Reginald Morton: but he went for a soldier, and was killed; and I never saw him more."

"Reginald Morton! What mean you, woman?—What know you of Reginald Morton?" demanded Wacousta, with frightful energy, as, leaning over the shrinking form of Clara, he violently grasped and shook the shoulder of the unhappy maniac.

"Stop; do not hurt me, and I will tell you all, sir," she almost screamed. "Oh, sir, Reginald Morton was my husband once; but he was kinder than you are. He did not look so fiercely at me; nor did he pinch me so."

"What of him?—who was he?" furiously repeated Wacousta, as he again impatiently shook the arm of the wretched Ellen. "Where did you know him?—Whence came he?"

"Nay, you must not be jealous of poor Reginald:" and, as she uttered these words in a softening and conciliating tone, her eye was turned upon those of the warrior with a mingled expression of fear and cunning. "But he was very good and very handsome, and generous; and we lived near each other, and we loved each other at first sight. But his family were very proud, and they quarrelled with him because he married me; and then we became very poor, and Reginald went for a soldier, and—; but I forget the rest, it is so long ago." She pressed her hand to her brow, and sank her head upon her chest.

"Ellen, woman, again I ask you where he came from? this Reginald Morton that you have named. To what county did he belong?"

"Oh, we were both Cornish," she answered, with a vivacity singularly in contrast with her recent low and monotonous tone; "but, as I said before, he was of a great family, and I only a poor clergyman's daughter."

"Cornish!—Cornish, did you say?" fiercely repeated the dark Wacousta, while an expression of loathing and disgust seemed for a moment to convulse his features; "then is it as I had feared. One word more. Was the family seat called Morton Castle?"

"It was," unhesitatingly returned the poor woman, yet with the air of one wondering to hear a name repeated, long forgotten even by herself. "It was a beautiful castle too, on a lovely ridge of hills; and it commanded such a nice view of the sea, close to the little port of ——; and the parsonage stood in such a sweet valley, close under the castle; and we were all so happy." She paused, again put her hand to her brow, and pressed it with force, as if endeavouring to pursue the chain of connection in her memory, but evidently without success.

"And your father's name was Clayton?" said the warrior, enquiringly; "Henry Clayton, if I recollect aright?"

"Ha! who names my father?" shrieked the wretched woman. "Yes, sir, it was Clayton—Henry Clayton—the kindest, the noblest of human beings. But the affliction of his child, and the persecutions of the Morton family, broke his heart. He is dead, sir, and Reginald is dead too; and I am a poor lone widow in the world, and have no one to love me."

131

Here the tears coursed each other rapidly down her faded cheek, although her eyes were staring and motionless.

"It is false!" vociferated the warrior, who, now he had gained all that was essential to the elucidation of his doubts, quitted the shoulder he had continued to press with violence in his nervous hand, and once more extended himself at his length; "in me you behold the uncle of your husband. Yes, Ellen Clayton, you have been the wife of two Reginald Mortons. Both," he pursued with unutterable bitterness, while he again started up and shook his tomahawk menacingly in the direction of the fort,—"both have been the victims of yon cold-blooded governor; but the hour of our reckoning is at hand. Ellen," he fiercely added, "do you recollect the curse you pronounced on the family of that haughty man, when he slaughtered your Reginald. By Heaven! it shall be fulfilled; but first shall the love I have so long borne the mother be transferred to the child."

Again he sought to encircle the waist of her whom, in the strong excitement of his rage, he had momentarily quitted; but the unutterable disgust and horror produced in the mind of the unhappy Clara lent an almost supernatural activity to her despair. She dexterously eluded his grasp, gained her feet, and with tottering steps and outstretched arms darted through the opening of the tent, and piteously exclaiming, "Save me! oh, for God's sake, save me!" sank exhausted, and apparently lifeless, on the chest of the prisoner without.

To such of our readers as, deceived by the romantic nature of the attachment stated to have been originally entertained by Sir Everard Valletort for the unseen sister of his friend, have been led to expect a tale abounding in manifestations of its progress when the parties had actually met, we at once announce disappointment. Neither the lover of amorous adventure, nor the admirer of witty dialogue, should dive into these pages. Room for the exercise of the invention might, it is true, be found; but ours is a tale of sad reality, and our heroes and heroines figure under circumstances that would render wit a satire upon the understanding, and love a reflection upon the heart. Within the bounds of probability have we, therefore, confined ourselves.

What the feelings of the young Baronet must have been, from the first moment when he received from the hands of the unfortunate Captain Baynton (who, although an officer of his own corps, was personally a stranger to him,) that cherished sister of his friend, on whose ideal form his excited imagination had so often latterly loved to linger, up to the present hour, we should vainly attempt to paint. There are emotions of the heart, it would be mockery in the pen to trace. From the instant of his first contributing to preserve her life, on that dreadful day of blood, to that when the schooner fell into the hands of the savages, few words had passed between them, and these had reference merely to the position in which they found themselves, and whenever Sir

Everard felt he could, without indelicacy or intrusion, render himself in the slightest way serviceable to her. The very circumstances under which they had met, conduced to the suppression, if not utter extinction, of all of passion attached to the sentiment with which he had been inspired. A new feeling had quickened in his breast; and it was with emotions more assimilated to friendship than to love that he now regarded the beautiful but sorrow-stricken sister of his bosom friend. Still there was a softness, a purity, a delicacy and tenderness in this new feeling, in which the influence of sex secretly though unacknowledgedly predominated; and even while sensible it would have been a profanation of every thing most sacred and delicate in nature to have admitted a thought of love within his breast at such a moment, he also felt he could have entertained a voluptuous joy in making any sacrifice, even to the surrender of life itself, provided the tranquillity of that gentle and suffering being could be by it ensured.

Clara, in her turn, had been in no condition to admit so exclusive a power as that of love within her soul. She had, it is true, even amid the desolation of her shattered spirit, recognised in the young officer the original of a portrait so frequently drawn by her brother, and dwelt on by herself. She acknowledged, moreover, the fidelity of the painting: but however she might have felt and acted under different circumstances, absorbed as was her heart, and paralysed her imagination, by the harrowing scenes she had gone through, she, too, had room but for one sentiment in her fainting soul, and that was friendship for the friend of her brother; on whom, moreover, she bestowed that woman's gratitude, which could not fail to be awakened by a recollection of the risks he had encountered, conjointly with Frederick, to save her from destruction. During their passage across lake Huron, Sir Everard had usually taken his seat on the deck, at that respectful distance which he conceived the delicacy of the position of the unfortunate cousins demanded; but in such a manner that, while he seemed wholly abstracted from them, his eye had more than once been detected by Clara fixed on hers, with an affectionateness of interest she could not avoid repaying with a glance of recognition and approval. These, however, were the only indications of regard that had passed between them.

If, however, a momentary and irrepressible flashing of that sentiment, which had, at an earlier period, formed a portion of their imaginings, did occasionally steal over their hearts while there was a prospect of reaching their friends in safety, all manifestation of its power was again finally suppressed when the schooner fell into the hands of the savages. Become the immediate prisoners of Wacousta, they had been surrendered to that ferocious chief to be dealt with as he might think proper; and, on disembarking from the canoe in which their transit to the main land had been descried that morning from the fort, had been separated from their equally unfortunate and suffering companions. Captain de Haldimar, Madeline, and the Canadian, were delivered over to the custody of several choice warriors of the tribe in which Wacousta was adopted; and, bound hand and foot, were, at that moment, in the war tent of the fierce savage, which, as Ponteac had once boasted to the governor, was every where hung around with human scalps, both of men, of women, and of children. The object of this mysterious man, in removing Clara to the spot we have described, was one well worthy of his ferocious nature. His vengeance had already devoted her to destruction; and it was within view of the fort, which contained the father whom he loathed, he had resolved his purpose should be accomplished. A refinement of cruelty, such as could scarcely have been supposed to enter the breast even of such a remorseless savage as himself, had caused him to convey to the same spot, him whom he rather suspected than knew to be the lover of the young girl. It was with the view of harrowing up the soul of one whom he had recognised as the officer who had disabled him on the night of the rencontre on the bridge, that he had bound Sir Everard to the tree, whence, as we have already stated, he was a compelled spectator of every thing that passed within the tent; and yet with that free action of limb which only tended to tantalize him the more amid his unavailable efforts to rid himself of his bonds,—a fact that proved not only the dire extent to which the revenge of Wacousta could be carried, but the actual and gratuitous cruelty of his nature.

One must have been similarly circumstanced, to understand all the agony of the young man during this odious scene, and particularly at the fierce and repeated declaration of the savage that Clara should be his bride. More than once had he essayed to remove the ligatures which confined his waist; but his unsuccessful attempts only drew an occasional smile of derision from his enemy, as he glanced his eye rapidly towards him. Conscious at length of the inutility of efforts, which, without benefiting her for whom they were principally prompted, rendered him in some degree ridiculous even in his own eyes, the wretched Valletort desisted altogether, and with his head sunk upon his chest, and his eyes closed, sought at least to shut out a scene which blasted his sight, and harrowed up his very soul.

But when Clara, uttering her wild cry for protection, and rushing forth from the tent, sank almost unconsciously in his embrace, a thrill of inexplicable joy ran through each awakened fibre of his frame. Bending eagerly forward, he had extended his arms to receive her; and when he felt her light and graceful form pressing upon his own as its last refuge—when he felt her heart beating against his—when he saw her head drooping on his shoulder, in the wild recklessness of despair,—even amid that scene of desolation and grief he could not help enfolding her in tumultuous ecstasy to his breast. Every horrible danger was for an instant forgotten in the soothing consciousness that he at length encircled the form of her, whom in many an hour of solitude he had thus pictured, although under far different circumstances, reposing confidingly on him. There was delight mingled with agony in his sensation of the wild throb of her bosom against his own; and even while his soul fainted within him, as he reflected on the fate that awaited her, he felt as if he could himself now die more happily.

Momentary, however, was the duration of this scene. Furious with anger at the evident disgust of his victim, Wacousta no sooner saw her sink into the arms of her lover, than with that agility for which he was remarkable he was again on his feet, and stood in the next instant at her side. Uniting to the generous strength of his manhood all that was wrung from his mingled love and despair, the officer clasped his hands round the waist of the drooping Clara; and with clenched teeth, and feet firmly set, seemed resolved to defy every effort of the warrior to remove her. Not a word was uttered on either side; but in the fierce smile that curled the lip of the savage, there spoke a language even more terrible than the words that smile implied. Sir Everard could not suppress an involuntary shudder; and when at length Wacousta, after a short but violent struggle, succeeded in again securing and bearing off his prize, the wretchedness of soul of the former was indescribable.

"You see 'tis vain to struggle against your destiny, Clara de Haldimar," sneered the warrior. "Ours is but a rude nuptial couch, it is true; but the wife of an Indian chief must not expect the luxuries of Europe in the heart of an American wilderness."

"Almighty Heaven! where am I?" exclaimed the wretched girl, again unclosing her eyes to all the horror of her position; for again she lay at the side, and within the encircling arm, of her enemy. "Oh, Sir Everard Valletort, I thought I was with you, and that you had saved me from this monster. Where is my brother?—Where are Frederick and Madeline?—Why have they deserted me?—Ah! my heart will break. I cannot endure this longer, and live."

"Clara, Miss de Haldimar," groaned Sir Everard, in a voice of searching agony; "could I lay down my life for you, I would; but you see these bonds. Oh God! oh God! have pity on the innocent; and for once incline the heart of yon fierce monster to the whisperings of mercy." As he uttered the last sentence, he attempted to sink on his knees in supplication to Him he addressed, but the tension of the cord prevented him; yet were his hands clasped, and his eyes upraised to heaven, while his countenance beamed with an expression of fervent enthusiasm.

"Peace, babbler! or, by Heaven! that prayer shall be your last," vociferated Wacousta. "But no," he pursued to himself,

139

dropping at the same time the point of his upraised tomahawk; "these are but the natural writhings of the crushed worm; and the longer protracted they are, the more complete will be my vengeance." Then turning to the terrified girl,—"You ask, Clara de Haldimar, where you are? In the tent of your mother's lover, I reply,—at the side of him who once pressed her to his heart, even as I now press you, and with a fondness that was only equalled by her own. Come, dear Clara," and his voice assumed a tone of tenderness that was even more revolting than his natural ferocity, "let me woo you to the affection she once possessed. It was a heart of fire in which her image stood enshrined,—it is a heart of fire still, and well worthy of her child."

"Never, never!" shrieked the agonised girl. "Kill me, murder me, if you will; but oh! if you have pity, pollute not my ear with the avowal of your detested love. But again I repeat, it is false that my mother ever knew you. She never could have loved so fierce, so vindictive a being as yourself."

"Ha! do you doubt me still?" sternly demanded the savage. Then drawing the shuddering girl still closer to his vast chest,—"Come hither, Clara, while to convince you I unfold the sad history of my life, and tell you more of your parents than you have ever known. When," he pursued solemnly, "you have learnt the extent of my love for the one, and of my hatred for the other, and the wrongs I have endured from both, you will no longer wonder at the spirit of mingled love

140

and vengeance that dictates my conduct towards yourself. Listen, girl," he continued fiercely, "and judge whether mine are injuries to be tamely pardoned, when a whole life has been devoted to the pursuit of the means of avenging them."

Irresistibly led by a desire to know what possible connection could have existed between her parents and this singular and ferocious man, the wretched girl gave her passive assent. She even hoped that, in the course of his narrative, some softening recollections would pass over his mind, the effect of which might be to predispose him to mercy. Wacousta buried his face for a few moments in his large hand, as if endeavouring to collect and concentrate the remembrances of past years. His countenance, meanwhile, had undergone a change; for there was now a shade of melancholy mixed with the fierceness of expression usually observable there. This, however, was dispelled in the course of his narrative, and as various opposite passions were in turn powerfully and severally developed.

CHAPTER VIII.

"It is now four and twenty years," commenced Wacousta, "since your father and myself first met as subalterns in the regiment he now commands, when, unnatural to say, an intimacy suddenly sprang up between us which, as it was then to our brother officers, has since been a source of utter astonishment to myself. Unnatural, I repeat, for fire and ice are not more opposite than were the elements of which our natures were composed. He, all coldness, prudence, obsequiousness, and forethought. I, all enthusiasm, carelessness, impetuosity, and independence. Whether this incongruous friendship—friendship! no, I will not so far sully the sacred name as thus to term the unnatural union that subsisted between us;—whether this intimacy, then, sprang from the adventitious circumstance of our being more frequently thrown together as officers of the same company,—for we were both attached to the grenadiers,—or that my wild spirit was soothed by the bland amenity of his manners, I know not. The latter, however, is not improbable; for proud, and haughty, and dignified, as the colonel NOW is, such was not THEN the character of the ensign; who seemed thrown out of one of Nature's supplest moulds, to fawn, and cringe, and worm his way to favour by the wily speciousness of his manners. Oh God!" pursued Wacousta, after a momentary pause, and striking his palm against his forehead, "that I ever should have been the dupe of such a cold-blooded hypocrite!

"I have said our intimacy excited surprise among our brother officers. It did; for all understood and read the character of your father, who was as much disliked and distrusted for the speciousness of his false nature, as I was generally esteemed for the frankness and warmth of mine. No one openly censured the evident preference I gave him in my friendship; but we were often sarcastically termed the Pylades and Orestes of the regiment, until my heart was ready to leap into my throat with impatience at the bitterness in which the taunt was conceived; and frequently in my presence was allusion made to the blind folly of him, who should take a cold and slimy serpent to his bosom only to feel its fangs darted into it at the moment when most fostered by its genial heat. All, however, was in vain. On a nature like mine, innuendo was likely to produce an effect directly opposite to that intended; and the more I found them inclined to be severe on him I called my friend, the more marked became my preference. I even fancied that because I was rich, generous, and heir to a title, their observations were prompted by jealousy of the influence he possessed over me, and a desire to supplant him only for their interests' sake. Bitterly have I been punished for the illiberality of such an opinion. Those to whom I principally allude were the subalterns of the regiment, most of whom were nearly of our own age. One or two of the junior captains were also of this number; but, by the elders (as we termed the seniors of that rank) and field officers, Ensign de Haldimar was always regarded as a most prudent and promising young officer.

143

"What conduced, in a great degree, to the establishment of our intimacy was the assistance I always received from my brother subaltern in whatever related to my military duties. As the lieutenant of the company, the more immediate responsibility attached to myself; but being naturally of a careless habit, or perhaps considering all duty irksome to my impatient nature that was not duty in the field, I was but too often guilty of neglecting it. On these occasions my absence was ever carefully supplied by your father, who, in all the minutiae of regimental economy, was surpassed by no other officer in the corps; so that credit was given to me, when, at the ordinary inspections, the grenadiers were acknowledged to be the company the most perfect in equipment and skilful in manoeuvre. Deeply, deeply," again mused Wacousta, "have these services been repaid.

"As you have just learnt, Cornwall is the country of my birth. I was the eldest of the only two surviving children of a large family; and, as heir to the baronetcy of the proud Mortons, was looked up to by lord and vassal as the future perpetuator of the family name. My brother had been designed for the army; but as this was a profession to which I had attached my inclinations, the point was waved in my favour, and at the age of eighteen I first joined the —— regiment, then quartered in the Highlands of Scotland. During my boyhood I had ever accustomed myself to athletic exercises, and loved to excite myself by encountering danger in its most terrific forms. Often had I passed whole days in climbing the steep and precipitous crags which overhang the sea in the neighbourhood of Morton Castle, ostensibly in the pursuit of the heron or the seagull, but self-acknowledgedly for the mere pleasure of grappling with the difficulties they opposed to me. Often, too, in the most terrific tempests, when sea and sky have met in one black and threatening mass, and when the startled fishermen have in vain attempted to dissuade me from my purpose, have I ventured, in sheer bravado, out of sight of land, and unaccompanied by a human soul. Then, when wind and tide have been against me on my return, have I, with my simple sculls alone, caused my faithful bark to leap through the foaming brine as though a press of canvass had impelled her on. Oh, that this spirit of adventure had never grown with my growth and strengthened with my strength!" sorrowfully added the warrior, again apostrophising himself: "then had I never been the wretch I am.

"The wild daring by which my boyhood had been marked was again powerfully awakened by the bold and romantic scenery of the Scottish Highlands; and as the regiment was at that time quartered in a part of these mountainous districts, where, from the disturbed nature of the times, society was difficult of attainment, many of the officers were driven from necessity, as I was from choice, to indulge in the sports of the chase. On one occasion a party of four of us set

145

out early in the morning in pursuit of deer, numbers of which we knew were to be met with in the mountainous tracts of Bute and Argyleshire. The course we happened to take lay through a succession of dark deep glens, and over frowning rocks; the difficulties of access to which only stirred up my dormant spirit of enterprise the more. We had continued in this course for many hours, overcoming one difficulty only to be encountered by another, and yet without meeting a single deer; when, at length, the faint blast of a horn was heard far above our heads in the distance, and presently a noble stag was seen to ascend a ledge of rocks immediately in front of us. To raise my gun to my shoulder and fire was the work of a moment, after which we all followed in pursuit. On reaching the spot where the deer had first been seen, we observed traces of blood, satisfying us he had been wounded; but the course taken in his flight was one that seemed to defy every human effort to follow in. It was a narrow pointed ledge, ascending boldly towards a huge cliff that projected frowningly from the extreme summit, and on either side lay a dark, deep, and apparently fathomless ravine; to look even on which was sufficient to appal the stoutest heart, and unnerve the steadiest brain. For me, however, long accustomed to dangers of the sort, it had no terror. This was a position in which I had often wished once more to find myself placed, and I felt buoyant and free as the deer itself I intended to pursue. In vain did my companions (and your father was one) implore me to abandon a project so wild and hazardous. I bounded forward, and they turned shuddering away, that their eyes might not witness the destruction that awaited me. Meanwhile, balancing my long gun in my upraised hands, I trod the dangerous path with a buoyancy and elasticity of limb, a lightness of heart, and a fearlessness of consequences, that surprised even myself. Perhaps it was to the latter circumstance I owed my safety, for a single doubt of my security might have impelled a movement that would not have failed to have precipitated me into the yawning gulf below. I had proceeded in this manner about five hundred yards, when I came to the termination of the ledge, from the equally narrow transverse extremity of which branched out three others; the whole contributing to form a figure resembling that of a trident. Pausing here for a moment, I applied the hunting horn, with which I was provided, to my lips. This signal, announcing my safety, was speedily returned by my friends below in a cheering and lively strain, that seemed to express at once surprise and satisfaction; and inspirited by the sound, I prepared to follow up my perilous chase. Along the ledge I had quitted I had remarked occasional traces where the stricken deer had passed; and the same blood-spots now directed me at a point where, but for these, I must have been utterly at fault. The centre of these new ridges, and the narrowest, was that taken by the animal, and on that I once more renewed my pursuit. As I continued to advance I found the ascent became more precipitous, and the difficulties opposed to my progress momentarily more multiplied. Still, nothing daunted, I continued my course towards the main body of rock that now rose within a hundred yards. How this was to be gained I knew not; for it shelved out abruptly from the extreme summit, overhanging the abyss, and presenting an appearance which I cannot more properly render than by comparing it to the sounding-boards placed over the pulpits of our English churches. Still I was resolved to persevere to the close, and I but too unhappily succeeded." Again Wacousta paused. A tear started to his eye, but this he impatiently brushed away with his swarthy hand.

"It was evident to me," he again resumed, "that there must be some opening through which the deer had effected his escape to the precipitous height above; and I felt a wild and fearful triumph in following him to his cover, over passes which it was my pleasure to think none of the hardy mountaineers themselves would have dared to venture upon with impunity. I paused not to consider of the difficulty of bearing away my prize, even if I succeeded in overtaking it. At every step my excitement and determination became stronger, and I felt every fibre of my frame to dilate, as when, in my more boyish days, I used to brave, in my gallant skiff, the mingled fury of the warring elements of sea and storm. Suddenly, while my mind was intent only on the dangers I used then to hold in such light estimation, I found my further progress intercepted by a fissure in the crag. It was not the width of this opening that disconcerted me, for it exceeded not ten feet; but I came upon it so unadvisedly, that, in attempting to check my forward motion, I had nearly lost my equipoise, and fallen into the abyss that now yawned before and on either side of me. To pause upon the danger, would, I felt, be to ensure it. Summoning all my dexterity into a single bound, I cleared the chasm; and with one buskined foot (for my hunting costume was strictly Highland) clung firmly to the ledge, while I secured my balance with the other. At this point the rock became gradually broader, so that I now trod the remainder of the rude path in perfect security, until I at length found myself close to the vast mass of which these ledges were merely ramifications or veins: but still I could discover no outlet by which the wounded deer could have escaped. While I lingered, thoughtfully, for a moment, half in disappointment, half in anger, and with my back leaning against the rock, I fancied I heard a rustling, as of the leaves and branches of underwood, on that part which projected like a canopy, far above the abyss. I bent my eye eagerly and fixedly on the spot whence the sound proceeded, and presently could distinguish the blue sky appearing through an aperture, to which was, the instant afterwards, applied what I conceived to be a human face. No sooner, however, was it seen than withdrawn; and then the rustling of leaves was heard again, and all was still as before.

"Why did my evil genius so will it," resumed Wacousta, after another pause, during which he manifested deep emotion, "that I should have heard those sounds and seen that face? But for these I should have returned to my companions, and my life might have been the life—the plodding life—of the multitude; things that are born merely to crawl through existence and die, knowing not at the moment of death why or how they have lived at all. But who may resist the destiny that presides over him from the cradle to the grave? for, although the mass may be, and are, unworthy of the influencing agency of that Unseen Power, who will presume to deny there are those on whom it stamps its iron seal, even from the moment of their birth to that which sees all that is mortal of them consigned to the tomb? What was it but destiny that whispered to me what I had seen was the face of a woman? I had not traced a feature, nor could I distinctly state that it was a human countenance I had beheld; but mine was ever an imagination into which the wildest improbability was scarce admitted that it did not grow into conviction in the instant.

"A new direction was now given to my feelings. I felt a presentiment that my adventure, if prosecuted, would terminate in some extraordinary and characteristic manner; and obeying, as I ever did, the first impulse of my heart, I prepared to grapple once more with the difficulties that yet remained to be surmounted. In order to do this, it was necessary that my feet and hands should be utterly without incumbrance; for it was only by dint of climbing that I could expect to reach that part of the projecting rock to which my attention had been directed. Securing my gun between some twisted roots that grew out of and adhered to the main body of the rock, I commenced the difficult ascent; and, after considerable effort, found myself at length immediately under the aperture. My progress along the lower superficies of this projection was like that of a crawling reptile. My back hung suspended over the chasm, into which one false movement of hand or foot, one yielding of the roots entwined in the rock, must inevitably have precipitated me; and, while my toes wormed themselves into the tortuous fibres of the latter, I passed hand over hand beyond my head, until I had arrived within a foot or two of the point I desired to reach. Here, however, a new difficulty occurred. A slight projection of the rock, close to the aperture, impeded my further progress in the manner hitherto pursued; and, to pass this, I was compelled to drop my whole weight, suspended by one vigorous arm, while, with the other, I separated the bushes that concealed the opening. A violent exertion of every muscle now impelled me upward, until at length I had so far succeeded as to introduce my head and shoulders through the aperture; after which my final success was no longer doubtful. If I have been thus minute in the detail of the dangerous nature of this passage," continued Wacousta, gloomily, "it is not without reason. I would have you to impress the whole of the localities upon your imagination, that you may the better comprehend, from a knowledge of the risks I incurred, how little I have merited the injuries under which I have writhed for years."

Again one of those painful pauses with which his narrative was so often broken, occurred; and, with an energy that terrified her whom he addressed, Wacousta pursued—"Clara de Haldimar, it was here—in this garden—this paradise—this oasis of the rocks in which I now found myself, that I first saw and loved your mother. Ha! you start: you believe me now.—Loved her!" he continued, after another short pause—"oh, what a feeble word is love to express the concentration of mighty feelings that flowed like burning lava through my veins! Who shall pretend to give a name to the emotion that ran thrillingly—madly through my excited frame, when first I gazed on her, who, in every attribute of womanly beauty, realised all my fondest fancy ever painted?—Listen to me, Clara," he pursued, in a fiercer tone, and with a convulsive pressure of the form he still encircled:—"If, in my younger days, my mind was alive to enterprise, and loved to contemplate danger in its most appalling forms, this was far from being the master passion of my soul; nay, it was the strong necessity I felt of pouring into some devoted bosom the overflowing fulness of my heart, that made me court in solitude those positions of danger with which the image of woman was ever associated.

How often, while tossed by the raging elements, now into the blue vault of heaven, now into the lowest gulfs of the sea, have I madly wished to press to my bounding bosom the being of my fancy's creation, who, all enamoured and given to her love, should, even amid the danger that environed her, be alive but to one consciousness,—that of being with him on whom her life's hope alone reposed! How often, too, while bending over some dark and threatening precipice, or standing on the utmost verge of some tall projecting cliff, my aching head (aching with the intenseness of its own conceptions) bared to the angry storm, and my eye fixed unshrinkingly on the boiling ocean far beneath my feet, has my whole soul—my every faculty, been bent on that ideal beauty which controlled every sense! Oh, imagination, how tyrannical is thy sway—how exclusive thy power—how insatiable thy thirst! Surrounded by living beauty, I was insensible to its influence; for, with all the perfection that reality can attain on earth, there was ever to be found some deficiency, either physical or moral, that defaced the symmetry and destroyed the loveliness of the whole; but, no sooner didst thou, with magic wand, conjure up one of thy embodiments, than my heart became a sea of flame, and was consumed in the vastness of its own fires.

"It was in vain that my family sought to awaken me to a sense of the acknowledged loveliness of the daughters of more than one ancient house in the county, with one of

153

whom an alliance was, in many respects, considered desirable. Their beauty, or rather their whole, was insufficient to stir up into madness the dormant passions of my nature; and although my breast was like a glowing furnace, in which fancy cast all the more exciting images of her coinage to secure the last impress of the heart's approval, my outward deportment to some of the fairest and loveliest of earth's realities was that of one on whom the influence of woman's beauty could have no power. From my earliest boyhood I had loved to give the rein to these feelings, until they at length rendered me their slave. Woman was the idol that lay enshrined within my inmost heart; but it was woman such as I had not yet met with, yet felt must somewhere exist in the creation. For her I could have resigned title, fortune, family, every thing that is dear to man, save the life, through which alone the reward of such sacrifice could have been tasted, and to this phantom I had already yielded up all the manlier energies of my nature; but, deeply as I felt the necessity of loving something less unreal, up to the moment of my joining the regiment, my heart had never once throbbed for created woman.

"I have already said that, on gaining the summit of the rock, I found myself in a sort of oasis of the mountains. It was so. Belted on every hand by bold and precipitous crags, that seemed to defy the approach even of the wildest animals, and putting utterly at fault the penetration and curiosity of man, was spread a carpet of verdure, a luxuriance of vegetation, that might have put to shame the fertility of the soft breeze-nourished valleys of Italy and Southern France. Time, however, is not given me to dwell on the mingled beauty and wildness of a scene, so consonant with my ideas of the romantic and the picturesque. Let me rather recur to her (although my heart be lacerated once more in the recollection) who was the presiding deity of the whole,—the being after whom, had I had the fabled power of Prometheus, I should have formed and animated the sharer of that sweet wild solitude, nor once felt that fancy, to whom I was so largely a debtor, had in aught been cheated of what she had, for a series of years, so rigidly claimed.

"At about twenty yards from the aperture, and on a bank, formed of turf, covered with moss, and interspersed with roses and honeysuckles, sat this divinity of the oasis. She, too, was clad in the Highland dress, which gave an air of wildness and elegance to her figure that was in classic harmony with the surrounding scenery. At the moment of my appearance she was in the act of dressing the wounded shoulder of a stag, that had recently been shot; and from the broad tartan riband I perceived attached to its neck, added to the fact of the tameness of the animal, I presumed that this stag, evidently a favourite of its mistress, was the same I had fired at and wounded. The rustling I made among the bushes had attracted her attention; she raised her eyes from

155

the deer, and, beholding me, started to her feet, uttering a cry of terror and surprise. Fearing to speak, as if the sound of my own voice were sufficient to dispel the illusion that fascinated both eye and heart into delicious tension on her form, yet with my soul kindled into all that wild uncontrollable love which had been the accumulation of years of passionate imagining, I stood for some moments as motionless as the rock out of which I appeared to grow. It seemed as though I had not the power to think or act, so fully was every faculty of my being filled with the consciousness that I at length gazed upon her I was destined to love for ever.

"It was this utter immobility on my own part, that ensured me a continuance of the exquisite happiness I then enjoyed. The first movement of the startled girl had been to fly towards her dwelling, which stood at a short distance, half imbedded in the same clustering roses and honey-suckles that adorned her bank of moss; but when she remarked my utter stillness, and apparent absence of purpose, she checked the impulse that would have directed her departure, and stopped, half in curiosity, half in fear, to examine me once more. At that moment all my energies appeared to be restored; I threw myself into an attitude expressive of deep contrition for the intrusion of which I had been unconsciously guilty, and dropping on one knee, and raising my clasped hands, inclined them towards her in token of mingled deprecation of her anger, and respectful homage to herself. At first she hesitated,—then gradually and timidly retrod her way to the seat she had so abruptly quitted in her alarm. Emboldened by this movement, I made a step or two in advance, but no sooner had I done so than she again took to flight. Once more, however, she turned to behold me, and again I had dropped on my knee, and was conjuring her, with the same signs, to remain and bless me with her presence. Again she returned to her seat, and again I advanced. Scarcely less timid, however, than the deer, which followed her every movement, she fled a third time,—a third time looked back, and was again induced, by my supplicating manner, to return. Frequently was this repeated, before I finally found myself at the feet, and pressing the hand—(oh God! what torture in the recollection!)—yes, pressing the hand of her for whose smile I would, even at that moment, have sacrificed my soul; and every time she fled, the classic disposition of her graceful limbs, and her whole natural attitude of alarm, could only be compared with those of one of the huntresses of Diana, intruded on in her woodland privacy by the unhallowed presence of some daring mortal. Such was your mother, Clara de Haldimar; yes, even such as I have described her was Clara Beverley."

Again Wacousta paused, and his pause was longer than usual, as, with his large hand again covering his face, he seemed endeavouring to master the feelings which these recollections had called up. Clara scarcely breathed. Unmindful of her own desolate position, her soul was intent only on a history that related so immediately to her beloved mother, of whom all that she had hitherto known was, that she was a native of Scotland, and that her father had married her while quartered in that country. The deep emotion of the terrible being before her, so often manifested in the course of what he had already given of his recital, added to her knowledge of the facts just named, scarcely left a doubt of the truth of his statement on her mind. Her ear was now bent achingly towards him, in expectation of a continuance of his history, but he still remained in the same attitude of absorption. An irresistible impulse caused her to extend her hand, and remove his own from his eyes: they were filled with tears; and even while her mind rapidly embraced the hope that this manifestation of tenderness was but the dawning of mercy towards the children of her he had once loved, her kind nature could not avoid sympathizing with him, whose uncouthness of appearance and savageness of nature was, in some measure, lost sight of in the fact of the powerful love he yet apparently acknowledged.

But no sooner did Wacousta feel the soft pressure of her hand, and meet her eyes turned on his with an expression of interest, than the most rapid transition was effected in his feelings. He drew the form of the weakly resisting girl closer to his heart; again imprinted a kiss upon her lips; and then, while every muscle in his iron frame seemed quivering with emotion, exclaimed,—"By Heaven! that touch, that glance, were Clara Beverley's all over! Oh, let me linger on the recollection, even such as they were, when her arms first opened to receive me in that sweet oasis of the Highlands. Yes, Clara," he proceeded more deliberately, as he scanned her form with an eye that made her shudder, "such as your mother was, so are you; the same delicacy of proportion; the same graceful curvature of limb, only less rounded, less womanly. But you must be younger by about two years than she then was. Your age cannot exceed seventeen; and time will supply what your mere girlhood renders you deficient in."

There was a cool licence of speech—a startling freedom of manner—in the latter part of this address, that disappointed not less than it pained and offended the unhappy Clara. It seemed to her as if the illusion she had just created, were already dispelled by his language, even as her own momentary interest in the fierce man had also been destroyed from the same cause. She shuddered; and sighing bitterly, suffered her tears to force themselves through her closed lids upon her pallid cheek. This change in her appearance seemed to act as a check on the temporary excitement of Wacousta. Again obeying one of these rapid transitions of feeling, for which he was remarkable, he once more assumed an expression of seriousness, and thus continued his narrative.

CHAPTER IX.

"It boots not now, Clara, to enter upon all that succeeded to my first introduction to your mother. It would take long to relate, not the gradations of our passion, for that was like the whirlwind of the desert, sudden and devastating from the first; but the burning vow, the plighted faith, the reposing confidence, the unchecked abandonment that flew from the lips, and filled the heart of each, sealed, as they were, with kisses, long, deep, enervating, even such as I had ever pictured that divine pledge of human affection should be. Yes, Clara de Haldimar, your mother was the child of nature THEN. Unspoiled by the forms, unvitiated by the sophistries of a world with which she had never mixed, her intelligent innocence made the most artless avowals to my enraptured ear,—avowals that the more profligate minded woman of society would have blushed to whisper even to herself. And for these I loved her to my own undoing.

"Blind vanity, inconceivable folly!" continued Wacousta, again pressing his forehead with force; "how could I be so infatuated as not to perceive, that although her heart was filled with a new and delicious passion, it was less the individual than the man she loved. And how could it be otherwise, since I was the first, beside her father, she had ever seen or recollected to have seen? Still, Clara de Haldimar," he pursued, with haughty energy, "I was not always the rugged being I now appear. Of surpassing strength I had ever been, and fleet of foot, but not then had I attained to my present gigantic stature; neither was my form endowed with the same Herculean rudeness; nor did my complexion wear the swarthy hue of the savage; nor had my features been rendered repulsive, from the perpetual action of those fierce passions which have since assailed my soul. My physical faculties had not yet been developed to their present grossness of maturity, neither had my moral energies acquired that tone of ferocity which often renders me hideous, even in my own eyes. In a word, the milk of my nature (for, with all my impetuosity of character, I was generous-hearted and kind) had not yet been turned to gall by villainy and deceit. My form had then all that might attract—my manners all that might win—my enthusiasm of speech all that might persuade—and my heart all that might interest a girl fashioned after nature's manner, and tutored in nature's school. In the regiment, I was called the handsome grenadier; but there was another handsomer than I,—a sly, insidious, wheedling, false, remorseless villain. That villain, Clara de Haldimar, was your father.

161

"But wherefore," continued Wacousta, chafing with the recollection, "wherefore do I, like a vain and puling schoolboy, enter into this abasing contrast of personal advantages? The proud eagle soars not more above the craven kite, than did my soul, in all that was manly and generous, above that of yon false governor; and who should have prized those qualities, if it were not the woman who, bred in solitude, and taught by fancy to love all that was generous and noble in the heart of man, should have considered mere beauty of feature as dust in the scale, when opposed to sentiments which can invest even deformity with loveliness? In all this I may appear vain; I am only just.

"I have said that your mother had been brought up in solitude, and without having seen the face of another man than her father. Such was the case;—Colonel Beverley, of English name, but Scottish connections, was an old gentleman of considerable eccentricity of character. He had taken a part in the rebellion of 1715; but sick and disgusted with an issue by which his fortunes had been affected, and heart-broken by the loss of a beloved wife, whose death had been accelerated by circumstances connected with the disturbed nature of the times, he had resolved to bury himself and child in some wild, where the face of man, whom he loathed, might no more offend his sight. This oasis of the mountains was the spot selected for his purpose; for he had discovered it some years previously, on an occasion, when, closely pursued by some of the English troops, and separated from his followers, he had only effected his escape by venturing on the ledges of rock I have already described. After minute subsequent search, at the opposite extremity of the oblong belt of rocks that shut it in on every hand, he had discovered an opening, through which the transport of such necessaries as were essential to his object might be effected; and, causing one of his dwelling houses to be pulled down, he had the materials carried across the rocks on the shoulders of the men employed to re-erect them in his chosen solitude. A few months served to complete these arrangements, which included a garden abounding in every fruit and flower that could possibly live in so elevated a region; and; this, in time, under his own culture, and that of his daughter, became the Eden it first appeared to me.

"Previous to their entering on this employment, the workmen had been severally sworn to secrecy; and when all was declared ready for his reception, the colonel summoned them a second time to his presence; when, after making a handsome present to each, in addition to his hire, he found no difficulty in prevailing on them to renew their oath that they would preserve the most scrupulous silence in regard to the place of his retreat. He then took advantage of a dark and tempestuous night to execute his project; and, attended only by an old woman and her daughter, faithful dependants of the family, set out in quest of his new abode, leaving all his neighbours to discuss and marvel at the singularity of his disappearance. True to his text, however, not even a boy was admitted into his household: and here they had continued to live, unseeing and unseen by man, except when a solitary and distant mountaineer occasionally flitted among the rocks below in pursuit of his game. Fruits and vegetables composed their principal diet; but once a fortnight the old woman was dispatched through the opening already mentioned, which was at other times so secured by her master, that no hand but his own could remove the intricate fastenings. This expedition had for its object the purchase of bread and animal food at the nearest market; and every time she sallied forth an oath was administered to the crone, the purport of which was, not only that she would return, unless prevented by violence or death, but that she would not answer any questions put to her, as to who she was, whence she came, or for whom the fruits of her marketing were intended.

"Meanwhile, wrapped up in his books, which were chiefly classic authors, or writers on abstruse sciences, the misanthropical colonel paid little or no attention to the cultivation of the intellect of his daughter, whom he had merely instructed in the elementary branches of education; in all which, however, she evinced an aptitude and perfectability that indicated quickness of genius and a capability of far higher attainments. Books he principally withheld from her, because they brought the image of man, whom he hated, and wished she should also hate, too often in flattering colours before her; and had any work treating of love been found to have crept accidentally into his own collection, it would instantly and indignantly have been committed to the flames.

"Thus left to the action of her own heart—the guidance of her own feelings—it was but natural your mother should have suffered her imagination to repose on an ideal happiness, which, although in some degree destitute of shape and character, was still powerfully felt. Nature is too imperious a law-giver to be thwarted in her dictates; and however we may seek to stifle it, her inextinguishable voice will make itself heard, whether it be in the lonely desert or in the crowded capital. Possessed of a glowing heart and warm sensibilities, Clara Beverley felt the energies of her being had not been given to her to be wasted on herself. In her dreams by night, and her thoughts by day, she had pictured a being endowed with those attributes which were the fruit of her own fertility of conception. If she plucked a flower, (and all this she admitted at our first interview," groaned Wacousta,) "she was sensible of the absence of one to whom that flower might be given. If she gazed at the star-studded canopy of heaven, or bent her head over the frowning precipices by which she was every where surrounded, she felt the absence of him with whom she could share the enthusiasm excited by

165

the contemplation of the one, and to whom she could impart the mingled terror and admiration produced by the dizzying depths of the other. What dear acknowledgments (alas! too deceitful,) flowed from her guileless lips, even during that first interview. With a candour and unreservedness that spring alone from unsophisticated manners and an untainted heart, she admitted, that the instant she beheld me, she felt she had found the being her fancy had been so long tutored to linger on, and her heart to love. She was sure I was come to be her husband (for she had understood from her aged attendant that a man who loved a woman wished to be her husband); and she was glad her pet stag had been wounded, since it had been the means of procuring her such happiness. She was not cruel enough to take pleasure in the sufferings of the poor animal; for she would nurse it, and it would soon be well again; but she could not help rejoicing in its disaster, since that circumstance had been the cause of my finding her out, and loving her even as she loved me. And all this was said with her head reclining on my chest, and her beautiful countenance irradiated with a glow that had something divine in the simplicity of purpose it expressed.

"On my demanding to know whether it was not her face I had seen at the opening in the cliff, she replied that it was. Her stag often played the truant, and passed whole hours away from her, rambling beyond the precincts of the solitude that contained its mistress; but no sooner was the small silver bugle, which she wore across her shoulder, applied to her lips, than 'Fidelity' (thus she had named him) was certain to obey the call, and to come bounding up the line of cliff to the main rock, into which it effected its entrance at a point that had escaped my notice. It was her bugle I had heard in the course of my pursuit of the animal; and, from the aperture through which I had effected my entrance, she had looked out to see who was the audacious hunter she had previously observed threading a passage, along which her stag itself never appeared without exciting terror in her bosom. The first glimpse she had caught of my form was at the moment when, after having sounded my own bugle, I cleared the chasm; and this was a leap she had so often trembled to see taken by 'Fidelity,' that she turned away and shuddered when she saw it fearlessly adventured on by a human being. A feeling of curiosity had afterwards induced her to return and see if the bold hunter had cleared the gulf, or perished in his mad attempt; but when she looked outward from the highest pinnacle of her rocky prison, she could discover no traces of him whatever. It then occurred to her, that, if successful in his leap, his progress must have been finally arrested by the impassable rock that terminated the ridge; in which case she might perchance obtain a nearer sight of his person. With this view she had removed the bushes enshrouding the aperture; and, bending low to the earth, thrust her head partially through it. Scarcely had she done so, however, when she beheld me

167

immediately, though far beneath her, with my back reposing against the rock, and my eyes apparently fixed on hers.

"Filled with a variety of opposite sentiments, among which unfeigned alarm was predominant, she had instantaneously removed her head; and, closing the aperture as noiselessly as possible, returned to the moss-covered seat on which I had first surprised her; where, while she applied dressings of herbs to the wound of her favourite, she suffered her mind to ruminate on the singularity of the appearance of a man so immediately in the vicinity of their retreat. The supposed impracticability of the ascent I had accomplished, satisfied, even while (as she admitted) it disappointed her. I must of necessity retrace my way over the dangerous ridge. Great, therefore, was her surprise, when, after having been attracted by the rustling noise of the bushes over the aperture, she presently saw the figure of the same hunter emerge from the abyss it overhung. Terror had winged her flight; but it was terror mingled with a delicious emotion entirely new to her. It was that emotion, momentarily increasing in power, that induced her to pause, look back, hesitate in her course, and finally be won, by my supplicating manner, to return and bless me with her presence.

"Two long and delicious hours," pursued Wacousta, after another painful pause of some moments, "did we pass in this manner; exchanging thought, and speech, and heart, as if the term of our acquaintance had been coeval with the first dawn of our intellectual life; when suddenly a small silver toned bell was heard from the direction of the house, hid from the spot—on which we sat by the luxuriant foliage of an intervening laburnum. This sound seemed to dissipate the dreamy calm that had wrapped the soul of your mother into forgetfulness. She started suddenly up, and bade me, if I loved her, begone; as that bell announced her required attendance on her father, who, now awakened from the mid-day slumber in which he ever indulged, was about to take his accustomed walk around the grounds; which was little else, in fact, than a close inspection of the walls of his natural castle. I rose to obey her; our eyes met, and she threw herself into my extended arms. We whispered anew our vows of eternal love. She called me her husband, and I pronounced the endearing name of wife. A burning kiss sealed the compact; and, on her archly observing that the sleep of her father continued about two hours at noon, and that the old woman and her daughter were always occupied within doors, I promised to repeat my visit every second day until she finally quitted her retreat to be my own for life. Again the bell was rung; and this time with a violence that indicated impatience of delay. I tore myself from her arms, darted to the aperture, and kissing my hand in reply to the graceful waving of her scarf as she half turned in her own flight, sunk finally from her view; and at length, after making the same efforts, and mastering the same obstacles that had marked and opposed my advance, once more found myself at the point whence I had set out in pursuit of the wounded deer.

"Many were the congratulations I received from my companions, whom I found waiting my return. They had endured the three hours of my absence with intolerable anxiety and alarm; until, almost despairing of beholding me again, they had resolved on going back without me. They said they had repeatedly sounded their horns; but meeting with no answer from mine, had been compelled to infer either that I had strayed to a point whence return to them was impracticable, or that I must have perished in the abyss. I readily gave in to the former idea; stating I had been led by the traces of the wounded deer to a considerable distance, and over passes which it had proved a work of time and difficulty to surmount, yet without securing my spoil. All this time there was a glow of animation on my cheek, and a buoyancy of spirit in my speech, that accorded ill, the first, with the fatigue one might have been supposed to experience in so perilous a chase; the second, with the disappointment attending its result. Your father, ever cool and quick of penetration, was the first to observe this; and when he significantly remarked, that, to judge from my satisfied countenance, my time had been devoted to the pursuit of more interesting game, I felt for a moment as if he was actually master of my secret, and was sensible my features underwent a change. I, however, parried the attack, by replying indifferently, that if he should have the hardihood to encounter the same dangers, he would, if successful, require no other prompter than the joy of self-preservation to lend the same glow of satisfaction to his own features. Nothing further was said on the subject; but conversing on indifferent topics, we again threaded the mazes of rock and underwood we had passed at an early hour, and finally gained the town in which we were quartered.

"During dinner, as on our way home, although my voice occasionally mixed with the voices of my companions, my heart was far away, and full of the wild but innocent happiness in which it had luxuriated. At length, the more freely to indulge in the recollection, I stole at an early hour from the mess-room, and repaired to my own apartments. In the course of the morning, I had hastily sketched an outline of your mother's features in pencil, with a view to assist me in the design of a miniature I purposed painting from memory. This was an amusement of which I was extremely and in which I had attained considerable excellence; being enabled, from memory alone, to give a most correct representation of any object that particularly fixed my attention. She had declared utter ignorance of the art herself, her father having studiously avoided instructing her in it from some unexplained motive; yet as she expressed the most unbounded admiration of those who possessed it, it was my intention to surprise her with a highly finished likeness of herself at my next visit. With this view I now set to work; and made such progress, that before I retired to rest I had completed all but the finishing touches, to which I purposed devoting a leisure hour or two by daylight on the morrow.

"While occupied the second day in its completion, it occurred to me I was in orders for duty on the following, which was that of my promised visit to the oasis; and I despatched my servant with my compliments to your father, and a request that he would be so obliging as to take my guard for me on the morrow, and I would perform his duty when next his name appeared on the roster. Some time afterwards I heard the door of the room in which I sat open, and some one enter. Presuming it to be my servant, returned from the execution of the message with which he had just been charged, I paid no attention to the circumstance; but finding, presently, he did not speak, I turned round with a view of demanding what answer he had brought. To my surprise, however, I beheld not my servant, but your father. He was standing looking over my shoulder at the work on which I was engaged; and notwithstanding in the instant he resumed the cold, quiet, smirking look that usually distinguished him, I thought I could trace the evidence of some deep emotion which my action had suddenly dispelled. He apologised for his intrusion, although we were on those terms that rendered apology unnecessary, but said he had just received my message, and preferred coming in person to assure me how happy he should feel to take my duty, or to render me any other service in his power. I thought he laid unusual emphasis on the last sentence; yet I thanked him warmly, stating that the only service I should now exact of him would be to take my guard, as I was compelled to be absent nearly the whole of the following morning. He observed, with a smile, he hoped I was not going to venture my neck on those dangerous precipices a second time, after the narrow escape I had had on the preceding day. As he spoke, I thought his eye met mine with a sly yet scrutinizing glance; and, not wishing to reply immediately to his question, I asked him what he thought of the work with which I was endeavouring to beguile an idle hour. He took it up, and I watched the expression of his handsome countenance with the anxiety of a lover who wishes that all should think his mistress beautiful as he does himself. It betrayed a very indefinite sort of admiration; and yet it struck me there was an eagerness in his dilating eye that contrasted strongly with the calm and unconcern of his other features. At length I asked him, laughingly, what he thought of my Cornish cousin. He replied, cautiously enough, that since it was the likeness of a cousin, and he dwelt emphatically on the word, he could not fail to admire it. Candour, however, compelled him to admit, that had I not declared the original to be one so closely connected with me,

173

he should have said the talent of so perfect an artist might have been better employed. Whatever, however, his opinion of the lady might be, there could be no question that the painting was exquisite; yet, he confessed, he could not but be struck with the singularity of the fact of a Cornish girl appearing in the full costume of a female Highlander. This, I replied, was mere matter of fancy and association, arising from my having been so much latterly in the habit of seeing that dress principally worn. He smiled one of his then damnable soft smiles of assent, and here the conversation terminated, and he left me.

"The next day saw me again at the side of your mother, who received me with the same artless demonstrations of affection. There was a mellowed softness in her countenance, and a tender languor in her eye, I had not remarked the preceding day. Then there was more of the vivacity and playfulness of the young girl; now, more of the deep fervour and the composed serenity of the thoughtful woman. This change was too consonant to my taste—too flattering to my self-love—not to be rejoiced in; and as I pressed her yielding form in silent rapture to my own, I more than ever felt she was indeed the being for whom my glowing heart had so long yearned. After the first full and unreserved interchange of our souls' best feelings, our conversation turned upon lighter topics; and I took an opportunity to produce the fruit of my application since we had parted. Never shall I forget the surprise and delight that animated her beautiful countenance when first she gazed upon the miniature. The likeness was perfect, even to the minutest shading of her costume; and so forcibly and even childishly did this strike her, that it was with difficulty I could persuade her she was not gazing on some peculiar description of mirror that reflected back her living image. She expressed a strong desire to retain it; and to this I readily assented: stipulating only to retain it until my next visit, in order that I might take an exact copy for myself. With a look of the fondest love, accompanied by a pressure on mine of lips that distilled dewy fragrance where they rested, she thanked me for a gift which she said would remind her, in absence, of the fidelity with which her features had been engraven on my heart. She admitted, moreover, with a sweet blush, that she herself had not been idle. Although her pencil could not call up my image in the same manner, her pen had better repaid her exertions; and, in return for the portrait, she would give me a letter she had written to beguile her loneliness on the preceding day. As she spoke she drew a sealed packet from the bosom of her dress, and placing it in my hand, desired me not to read it until I had returned to my home. But there was an expression of sweet confusion in her lovely countenance, and a trepidation in her manner, that, half disclosing the truth, rendered me utterly impatient of the delay imposed; and eagerly breaking the seal, I devoured rather than read its contents.

"Accursed madness of recollection!" pursued Wacousta, again striking his brow violently with his hand,—"why is it that I ever feel thus unmanned while recurring to those letters? Oh! Clara de Haldimar, never did woman pen to man such declarations of tenderness and attachment as that too dear but faithless letter of your mother contained. Words of fire, emanating from the guilelessness of innocence, glowed in every line; and yet every sentence breathed an utter unconsciousness of the effect those words were likely to produce. Mad, wild, intoxicated, I read the letter but half through; and, as it fell from my trembling hand, my eye turned, beaming with the fires of a thousand emotions, upon that of the worshipped writer. That glance was more than her own could meet. A new consciousness seemed to be stirred up in her soul. Her eye dropped beneath its long and silken fringe—her cheek became crimson—her bosom heaved—and, all confidingness, she sank her head upon my chest, which heaved scarcely less wildly than her own.

"Had I been a cold-blooded villain—a selfish and remorseless seducer," continued Wacousta with vehemence—"what was to have prevented my triumph at that moment? But I came not to blight the flower that had long been nurtured, though unseen, with the life-blood of my own being. Whatever I may be NOW, I was THEN the soul of disinterestedness and honour; and had she reposed on the bosom of her own father, that devoted and unresisting girl could not have been pressed there with holier tenderness. But even to this there was too soon a term. The hour of parting at length arrived, announced, as before, by the small bell of her father, and I again tore myself from her arms; not, however, without first securing the treasured letter, and obtaining a promise from your mother that I should receive another at each succeeding visit."

CHAPTER X.

"Nearly a month passed away in this manner; and at each interview our affection seemed to increase. The days of our meeting were ever days of pure and unalloyed happiness; while the alternate ones of absence were, on my part, occupied chiefly with reading the glowing letters given me at each parting by your mother. Of all these, however, there was not one so impassioned, so natural, so every way devoted, as the first. Not that she who wrote them felt less, but that the emotion excited in her bosom by the manifestation of mine on that occasion, had imparted a diffidence to her style of expression, plainly indicating the source whence it sprung.

"One day, while preparing to set out on my customary excursion, a report suddenly reached me that the route had arrived for the regiment, who were to march from —— within three days. This intelligence I received with inconceivable delight; for it had been settled between your mother and myself, that this should be the moment chosen for her departure. It was not to be supposed (and I should have been both pained and disappointed had it been otherwise,) that she would consent to abandon her parent without some degree of regret; but, having foreseen this objection from the first, I had gradually prepared her for the sacrifice. This was the less difficult, as he appeared never to have treated her with affection,—seldom with the marked favour that might have been presumed to distinguish the manner of a father towards a lovely and only daughter. Living for himself and the indulgence of his misanthropy alone, he cared little for the immolation of his child's happiness on its unhallowed shrine; and this was an act of injustice I had particularly dwelt upon; upheld in truth, as it was, by the knowledge she herself possessed, that no consideration could induce him to bestow her hand on any one individual of a race he so cordially detested; and this was not without considerable weight in her decision.

"With a glowing cheek, and a countenance radiant with happiness, did your mother receive my proposal to prepare for her departure on the following day. She was sufficiently aware, even through what I had stated myself, that there were certain ceremonies of the Church to be performed, in order to give sanctity to our union, and ensure her own personal respectability in the world; and these, I told her, would be solemnised by the chaplain of the regiment. She implicitly confided in me; and she was right; for I loved her too well to make her my mistress, while no barrier existed to her claim to a dearer title. And had she been the daughter of a peasant, instead of a high-born gentleman, finding her as I had found her, and loving her as I did love her, I should have acted precisely in the same way.

"The only difficulty that now occurred was the manner of her flight. The opening before alluded to as being the point whence the old woman made her weekly sally to the market town, was of so intricate and labyrinthian a character that none but the colonel understood the secret of its fastenings; and the bare thought of my venturing with her on the route by which I had hitherto made my entry into the oasis, was one that curdled my blood with fear. I could absolutely feel my flesh to contract whenever I painted the terrible risk that would be incurred in adopting a plan I had once conceived,—namely, that of lashing your mother to my back, while I again effected my descent to the ledge beneath, in the manner I had hitherto done. I felt that, once on the ridge, I might, without much effort, attain the passage of the fissure already described; for the habit of accomplishing this leap had rendered it so perfectly familiar to me, that I now performed it with the utmost security and ease; but to imagine our united weight suspended over the abyss, as it necessarily must be in the first stage of our flight, when even the dislodgment of a single root or fragment of the rock was sufficient to ensure the horrible destruction of her whom I loved better than my own life, had something too appalling in it to suffer me to dwell on the idea for more than a moment. I had proposed, as the most feasible and rational plan, that the colonel should be compelled to give us egress through the secret passage, when we might command the services of the old woman to guide us through the passes that led to the town; but to this your mother most urgently objected, declaring that she would rather encounter any personal peril that might attend her escape, in a different manner, than appear to be a participator in an act of violence against her parent whose obstinacy of character she moreover knew too well to leave a hope of his being intimidated into the accomplishment of our object, even by a threat of death itself. This plan I was therefore compelled to abandon; and as neither of us were able to discover the passage by which the deer always effected its entrance, I was obliged to fix upon one, which it was agreed should be put in practice on the following day.

"On my return, I occupied myself with preparations for the reception of her who was so speedily to become my wife. Unwilling that she should be seen by any of my companions, until the ceremony was finally performed, I engaged apartments in a small retired cottage, distant about half a mile from the furthest extremity of the town, where I purposed she should remain until the regiment finally quitted the station. This point secured, I hastened to the quarters of the chaplain, to engage his services for the following evening; but he was from home at the time, and I repaired to my own rooms, to prepare the means of escape for your mother. These occupied me until a very late hour; and when at length I retired to rest, it was only to indulge in the fondest imaginings that ever filled the heart of a devoted lover. Alas! (and the dark warrior again sighed heavily) the day-dream of my happiness was already fast drawing to a close.

"At half an hour before noon, I was again in the oasis; your mother was at the wonted spot; and although she received me with her sunniest smiles, there were traces of tears upon her cheek. I kissed them eagerly away, and sought to dissipate the partial gloom that was again clouding her brow. She observed it pained me to see her thus, and she made a greater effort to rally. She implored me to forgive her weakness; but it was the first time she was to be separated from her parent; and conscious as she was that it was to be for ever, she could not repress the feeling that rose, despite of herself, to her heart. She had, however, prepared a letter, at my suggestion, to be left on her favourite moss seat, where it was likely she would first be sought by her father, to assure him of her safety, and of her prospects of future happiness; and the consciousness that he would labour under no harrowing uncertainty in regard to her fate, seemed, at length, to soothe and satisfy her heart.

"I now led her to the aperture, where I had left the apparatus provided for my purpose: this consisted of a close netting, about four feet in depth, with a board for a footstool at the bottom, and furnished at intervals with hoops, so as to keep it full and open. The top of this netting was provided with two handles, to which were attached the ends of a cord many fathoms in length; the whole of such durability, as to have borne weights equal to those of three ordinary sized men, with which I had proved it prior to my setting out. My first care was to bandage the eyes of your mother, (who willingly and fearlessly submitted to all I proposed,) that she might not see, and become faint with seeing, the terrible chasm over which she was about to be suspended. I then placed her within the netting, which, fitting closely to her person, and reaching under her arms, completely secured her; and my next urgent request was, that she would not, on any account, remove the bandage, or make the slightest movement, when she found herself stationary below, until I had joined her. I then dropped her gently through the aperture, lowering fathom after fathom of the rope, the ends of which I had firmly secured round the trunk of a tree, as an additional safeguard, until she finally came on a level with that part of the cliff on which I had reposed when first she beheld me. As she still hung immediately over the abyss, it was necessary to give a gradual impetus to her weight, to enable her to gain the landing-place. I now, therefore, commenced swinging her to and fro, until she at length came so near the point desired, that I clearly saw the principal difficulty was surmounted. The necessary motion having been given to the balance, with one vigorous and final impulsion I dexterously contrived to deposit her several feet from the edge of the lower rock, when, slackening the rope on the instant, I had the inexpressible satisfaction to see that she remained firm and stationary. The waving of her scarf immediately afterwards (a signal previously agreed upon), announced she had sustained no injury in this rather rude collision with the rock, and I in turn commenced my descent.

"Fearing to cast away the ends of the rope, lest their weight should by any chance effect the balance of the footing your mother had obtained, I now secured them around my loins, and accomplishing my descent in the customary manner, speedily found myself once more at the side of my heart's dearest treasure. Here the transport of my joy was too great to be controlled; I felt that NOW my prize was indeed secured to me for ever; and I burst forth into the most passionate exclamations of tenderness, and falling on my knees, raised my hands to Heaven in fervent gratitude for the success with which my enterprise had been crowned.

Another would have been discouraged at the difficulties still remaining; but with these I was become too familiar, not to feel the utmost confidence in encountering them, even with the treasure that was equally perilled with myself. For a moment I removed the bandage from the eyes of your mother, that she might behold not only the far distant point whence she had descended, but the frowning precipice I had daily been in the habit of climbing to be blest with her presence. She did so,—and her cheek paled, for the first time, with a sense of the danger I had incurred; then turning her soft and beautiful eyes on mine, she smiled a smile that seemed to express how much her love would repay me. Again our lips met, and we were happy even in that lonely spot, beyond all language to describe. Once more, at length, I prepared to execute the remainder of my task; and I again applied the bandage to her eyes, saying that, although the principal danger was over, still there was another I could not bear she should look upon. Again she smiled, and with a touching sweetness of expression that fired my blood, observing at the same time she feared no danger while she was with me, but that if my object was to prevent her from looking at me, the most efficient way certainly was to apply a bandage to her eyes. Oh! woman, woman!" groaned Wacousta, in fierce anguish of spirit, "who shall expound the complex riddle of thy versatile nature?

"Disengaging the rope from the handles of the netting, I now applied to these a broad leathern belt taken from the pouches of two of my men, and stooping with my back to the cherished burden with which I was about to charge myself, passed the centre of the belt across my chest, much in the manner in which, as you are aware, Indian women carry their infant children. As an additional precaution, I had secured the netting round my waist by a strong lacing of cord, and then raising myself to my full height, and satisfying myself of the perfect freedom of action of my limbs, seized a long balancing pole I had left suspended against the rock at my last visit, and commenced my descent of the sloping ridge. On approaching the horrible chasm, a feeling of faintness came over me, despite of the confidence with which I had previously armed myself. This, however, was but momentary. Sensible that every thing depended on rapidity of movement, I paused not in my course; but, quickening my pace as I gradually drew nearer, gave the necessary impetus to my motion, and cleared the gap with a facility far exceeding what had distinguished my first passage, and which was the fruit of constant practice alone. Here my balance was sustained by the pole; and at length I had the inexpressible satisfaction to find myself at the very extremity of the ridge, and immediately at the point where I had left my companions in my first memorable pursuit. Alas!" continued the warrior, again interrupting himself with one of those fierce exclamations of impatient anguish that so frequently occurred in his narrative, "what subject for rejoicing was there in this? Better far we had been dashed to pieces in the abyss, than I should have lived to curse the hour when first my spirit of adventure led me to traverse it." Again he resumed:—

"In the deep transport of my joy, I once more threw myself on my knees in speechless thanksgiving to Providence for the complete success of my undertaking. Your mother, whom I had previously released from her confinement, did the same; and at that moment the union of our hearts seemed to be cemented by a divine influence, manifested in the fulness of the gratitude of each. I then raised her from the earth, imprinting a kiss upon her fair brow, that was hallowed by the purity of the feeling I had so recently indulged in; and throwing over her shoulders the mantle of a youth, which I had secreted near the spot, enjoined her to follow me closely in the path I was about to pursue. As she had hitherto encountered no fatigue, and was, moreover, well provided with strong buskins I had brought for the purpose, I thought it advisable to discontinue the use of the netting, which must attract notice, and cause us, perhaps, to be followed, in the event of our being met by any of the hunters that usually traversed these parts. To carry her in my arms, as I should have preferred, might have excited the same curiosity, and I was therefore compelled to decide upon her walking; reserving to myself, however, the sweet task of bearing her in my embrace over the more difficult parts of our course.

"I have not hitherto found it necessary to state," continued Wacousta, his brow lowering with fierce and gloomy thought, "that more than once, latterly, on my return from the oasis, which was usually at a stated hour, I had observed a hunter hovering near the end of the ledge, yet quickly retreating as I advanced. There was something in the figure of this man that recalled to my recollection the form of your father; but ever, on my return to quarters, I found him in uniform, and exhibiting any thing but the appearance of one who had recently been threading his weary way among rocks and fastnesses. Besides, the improbability of this fact was so great, that it occupied not my attention beyond the passing moment. On the present occasion, however, I saw the same hunter, and was more forcibly than ever struck by the resemblance to my friend. Prior to my quitting the point where I had liberated your mother from the netting, I had, in addition to the disguise of the cloak, found it necessary to make some alteration in the arrangement of her hair; the redundancy of which, as it floated gracefully over her polished neck, was in itself sufficient to betray her sex. With this view I had removed her plumed bonnet. It was the first time I had seen her without it; and so deeply impressed was I by the angel-like character of the extreme feminine beauty she, more than ever, then exhibited, that I knelt in silent adoration for some moments at her feet, my eyes and countenance alone expressing the fervent and almost holy emotion of my enraptured soul. Had she been a divinity, I could not have worshipped her with a purer feeling. While I yet knelt, I fancied I heard a sound behind me; and, turning quickly, beheld the head of a man peering above a point of rock at some little distance. He immediately, on witnessing my action, sank again beneath it, but not in sufficient time to prevent my almost assuring myself that it was the face of your father I had beheld. My first impulse was to bound forward, and satisfy myself who it really was who seemed thus ever on the watch to intercept my movements; but a second rapid reflection convinced me, that, having been discovered, it was most likely the intruder had already effected his retreat, and that any attempt at pursuit might not only alarm your mother, but compromise her safety. I determined, however, to tax your father with the fact on my return to quarters; and, from the manner in which he met the charge, to form my own conclusion.

"Meanwhile we pursued our course; and after an hour's rather laborious exertion, at length emerged from the succession of glens and rocks that lay in our way; when, skirting the valley in which the town was situated, we finally reached the cottage where I had secured my lodging. Previous to entering it, I had told your mother, that for the few hours that would intervene before the marriage ceremony could be performed, I should, by way of lulling the curiosity of her hostess, introduce her as a near relative of my own. This I did accordingly; and, having seen that every thing was comfortably arranged for her convenience, and recommending her strongly to the care of the old woman, I set off once more in search of the chaplain of the regiment Before I could reach his residence, however, I was met by a sergeant of my company, who came running towards me, evidently with some intelligence of moment. He stated, that my presence was required without delay. The grenadiers, with the senior subaltern, were in orders for detachment for an important service; and considerable displeasure had been manifested by the colonel at my absence, especially as of late I had greatly neglected my military duties. He had been looking for me every where, he said, but without success, when Ensign de Haldimar had pointed out to him in what direction it was likely I might be found.

"At a calmer moment, I should have been startled at the last observation; but my mind was too much engrossed with the principal subject of my regret, to pay any attention to the circumstance. It was said the detachment would be occupied in this duty a week or ten days, at least; and how was I to absent myself from her whom I so fondly loved for this period, without even being permitted first to see and account to her for my absence? There was torture in the very thought; and in the height of my impatience, I told the sergeant he might give my compliments to the colonel, and say I would see the service d—d rather than inconvenience myself by going out on this duty at so short a notice; that I had private business of the highest importance to myself to transact, and could not absent myself. As the man, however, prepared coolly to depart, it suddenly occurred to me, that I might prevail on your father to take my duty now, as on former occasions he had willingly done, and I countermanded my message to the colonel; desiring him, however, to find out Ensign de Haldimar, and say that I requested to see him immediately at my quarters, whither I was now proceeding to change my dress.

"With a beating heart did I assume an uniform that appeared, at that moment, hideous in my eyes; yet I was not without a hope I might yet get off this ill-timed duty. Before I had completed my equipment, your father entered; and when I first glanced my eye full upon his, I thought his countenance exhibited evidences of confusion. This immediately reminded me of the unknown hunter, and I asked him if he was not the person I described. His answer was not a positive denial, but a mixture of raillery and surprise that lulled my doubts, enfeebled as they were by the restored calm of his features. I then told him that I had a particular favour to ask of him, which, in consideration of our friendship, I trusted he would not refuse; and that was, to take my duty in the expedition about to set forth. His manner implied concern; and he asked, with a look that had much deliberate expression in it, 'if I was aware that it was a duty in which blood was expected to be shed? He could not suppose that any consideration would induce me to resign my duty to another officer, when apprised of this fact.' All this was said with the air of one really interested in my honour; but in my increasing impatience, I told him I wanted none of his cant; I simply asked him a favour, which he would grant or decline as he thought proper. This was a harshness of language I had never indulged in; but my mind was sore under the existing causes of my annoyance, and I could not bear to have my motives reflected on at a moment when my heart was torn with all the agonies attendant on the position in which I found myself placed. His cheek paled and flushed more than once, before he replied, 'that in spite of my unkindness his friendship might induce him to do much for me, even as he had hitherto done, but that on the present occasion it rested not with him. In order to justify himself he would no longer disguise the fact from me, that the colonel had declared, in the presence of the whole regiment, I should take my duty regularly in future, and not be suffered to make a convenience of the service any longer. If, however, he could do any thing for me during my absence, I had but to command him.

"While I was yet giving vent, in no very measured terms, to the indignation I felt at being made the subject of public censure by the colonel, the same sergeant came into the room, announcing that the company were only waiting for me to march, and that the colonel desired my instant presence. In the agitation of my feelings, I scarcely knew what I did, putting several portions of my regimental equipment on so completely awry, that your father noticed and rectified the errors I had committed; while again, in the presence of the sergeant, I expressed the deepest regret he could not relieve me from a duty that was hateful to the last degree.

"Torn with agony at the thought of the uncertainty in which I was compelled to leave her, whom I so fondly adored, I had now no other alternative than to make a partial confidant of your father. I told him that in the cottage which I pointed out he would find the original of the portrait he had seen me painting on a former occasion,—the Cornish cousin, whose beauty he professed to hold so cheaply. More he should know of her on my return; but at present I confided her to his honour, and begged he would prove his friendship for me by rendering her whatever attention she might require in her humble abode. With these hurried injunctions he promised to comply; and it has often occurred to me since, although I did not remark it at the time, that while his voice and manner were calm, there was a burning glow upon his handsome cheek, and a suppressed exultation in his eye, that I had never observed on either before. I then quitted the room; and hastening to my company with a gloom on—my brow that indicated the wretchedness of my inward spirit, was soon afterwards on the march from ——."

Again the warrior seemed agitated with the most violent emotion; he buried his face in his hands; and the silence that ensued was longer than any he had previously indulged in. At length he made an effort to arouse himself; and again exhibiting his swarthy features, disclosed a brow, not clouded, as before, by grief, but animated with the fiercest and most appalling passions, while he thus impetuously resumed.

CHAPTER XI.

"If, hitherto, Clara de Haldimar, I have been minute in the detail of all that attended my connection with your mother, it has been with a view to prove to you how deeply I have been injured; but I have now arrived at a part of my history, when to linger on the past would goad me into madness, and render me unfit for the purpose to which I have devoted myself. Brief must be the probing of wounds, that nearly five lustres have been insufficient to heal; brief the tale that reveals the infamy of those who have given you birth, and the utter blighting of the fairest hopes of one whose only fault was that of loving, "not too wisely, but too well."

"Will you credit the monstrous truth," he added, in a fierce but composed whisper, while he bent eagerly over the form of the trembling yet attentive girl, "when I tell you that, on my return from that fatal expedition, during my continuance on which her image had never once been absent from my mind, I found Clara Beverley the wife of De Haldimar? Yes," continued Wacousta, his wounded feeling and mortified pride chafing, by the bitter recollection, into increasing fury, while his countenance paled in its swarthiness, "the wife, the wedded wife of yon false and traitorous governor! Well may you look surprised, Clara de Haldimar: such damnable treachery as this may startle his own blood in the veins of another, nor find its justification even in the devotedness of woman's filial piety. To what satanic arts so calculating a villain could have had recourse to effect his object I know not; but it is not the less true, that she, from whom my previous history must have taught you to expect the purity of intention and conduct of an angel, became his wife,—and I a being accursed among men. Even as our common mother is said to have fallen in the garden of Eden, tempted by the wily beauty of the devil, so did your mother fall, seduced by that of the cold, false, traitorous De Haldimar." Here the agitation of Wacousta became terrific. The labouring of his chest was like that of one convulsed with some racking agony and the swollen veins and arteries of his head seemed to threaten the extinction of life in some fearful paroxysm. At length he burst into a violent fit of tears, more appalling, in one of his iron nature, than the fury which had preceded it,—and it was many minutes before he could so far compose himself as to resume.

"Think not, Clara de Haldimar, I speak without the proof. Her own words confessed, her own lips avowed it, and yet I neither slew her, nor her paramour, nor myself. On my return to the regiment I had flown to the cottage, on the wings of the most impatient and tender love that ever filled the bosom of man for woman. To my enquiries the landlady replied, that my cousin had been married two days previously, by the military chaplain, to a handsome young officer, who had visited her soon after my departure, and was constantly with her from that moment; and that immediately after the ceremony they had left, but she knew not whither. Wild, desperate, almost bereft of reason, and with a heart bounding against my bosom, as if each agonising throb were to be its last, I ran like a maniac back into the town, nor paused till I found myself in the presence of your father. My mind was a volcano, but still I attempted to be calm, even while I charged him, in the most outrageous terms, with his villainy. Deny it he could not; but, far from excusing it, he boldly avowed and justified the step he had taken, intimating, with a smile full of meaning, there was nothing in a connection with the family of De Haldimar to reflect disgrace on the cousin of Sir Reginald Morton; and that; the highest compliment he could pay his friend was to attach himself to one whom that friend had declared to be so near a relative of his own. There was a coldness of taunt in these remarks, that implied his sense of the deception I had practised on him, in regard to the true nature of the relationship; and for a moment, while my hand firmly grasped the hilt of my sword, I hesitated whether I should not cut him down at my feet: I had self-command, however, to abstain from the outrage, and I have often since regretted I had. My own blood could have been but spilt in atonement for my just revenge; and as for the obloquy attached to the memory of the assassin, it could not have been more bitter than that which has followed me through life. But what do I say?" fiercely continued the warrior, an exulting ferocity sparkling in his eye, and animating his countenance; "had he fallen, then my vengeance were but half complete. No; it is now he shall feel the deadly venom in his heart, that has so long banqueted on mine.

"Determined to know from her own lips," he pursued, to the shuddering Clara, whose hopes, hitherto strongly excited, now, began again to fade beneath the new aspect given to the strange history of this terrible man;— "determined to satisfy myself from her own acknowledgment, whether all I had heard was not an imposition, I summoned calmness enough to desire that your mother might confirm in person the alienation of her affection, as nothing short of that could convince me of the truth. He left the room, and presently re-appeared, conducting her in from another: I thought she looked more beautiful than ever, but, alas! I had the inexpressible horror to discover, before a word was uttered, that all the fondness of her nature was indeed transferred to your father. How I endured the humiliation of that scene has often been a source of utter astonishment to myself; but I did endure it. To my wild demand, how she could so soon have forgotten her vows, and falsified her plighted engagements, she replied, timidly and confusedly, she had not yet known her own heart; but if she had pained me by her conduct, she was sorry for it, and hoped I would forgive her. She would always be happy to esteem me as a friend, but she loved her Charles far, far better than she had ever loved me. This damning admission, couched in the same language of simplicity that had first touched and won my affection, was like boiling lead upon my brain. In a transport of madness I sprang towards her, caught her in my arms, and swore she should accompany me back to the oasis—when I had taken her there, to be regained by my detested rival, if he could; but that he should not eat the fruit I had plucked at so much peril to myself. She struggled to disengage herself, calling on your father by the most endearing epithets to free her from my embrace. He attempted it, and I struck him senseless to the

197

floor at a single blow with the flat of my sabre, which in my extreme fury I had unsheathed. Instead, however, of profiting by the opportunity thus afforded to execute my threat, a feeling of disgust and contempt came over me, for the woman, whose inconstancy had been the cause of my committing myself in this ungentlemanly manner; and bestowing deep but silent curses on her head, I rushed from the house in a state of frenzy. How often since have I regretted that I had not pursued my first impulse, and borne her to some wild, where, forgetting one by whose beauty of person her eye alone had been seduced, her heart might have returned to its allegiance to him who had first awakened the sympathies of her soul, and would have loved her with a love blending the fiercest fires of the eagle with the gentlest devotedness of the dove. But destiny had differently ordained.

"Did my injuries end here?" pursued the dark warrior, as his eye kindled with rage. "No: for weeks I was insensible to any thing but the dreadful shock my soul had sustained. A heavy stupor weighed me down, and for a period it was supposed my reason was overthrown: no such mercy was reserved for me. The regiment had quitted the Highlands, and were now stationary in ——, whither I had accompanied it in arrest. The restoration of my faculties was the signal for new persecutions. Scarcely had the medical officers reported me fit to sustain the ordeal, when a court-martial was assembled to try me on a variety of charges. Who was my prosecutor? Listen, Clara," and he shook her violently by the arm. "He who had robbed me of all that gave value to life, and incentive to honour,—he who, under the guise of friendship, had stolen into the Eden of my love, and left it barren of affection. In a word, yon detested governor, to whose inhuman cruelty even the son of my brother has, by some strange fatality of coincidence, so recently fallen a second sacrifice. Curses, curses on him," he pursued, with frightful vehemence, half rising as he spoke, and holding forth his right arm in a menacing attitude; "but the hour of retribution is at hand, and revenge, the exclusive passion of the gods, shall at length be mine. In no other country in the world—under no other circumstances than the present—could I have so secured it.

"What were the charges preferred against me?" he continued, with a violence that almost petrified the unhappy girl. "Hear them, and judge whether I have not cause for the inextinguishable hate that rankles at my heart. Every trifling disobedience of orders—every partial neglect of duty that could be raked up—was tortured into a specific charge; and, as I have already admitted I had latterly transgressed not a little in this respect, these were numerous enough. Yet they were but preparatory to others of greater magnitude. Next succeeded one that referred to the message I had given, and countermanded, to the sergeant of my company, when in the impatience of my disappointment I had desired him to tell the colonel I would see the service d—d rather than inconvenience myself at that moment for it. This was unsupported by other evidence, however, and therefore failed in the proof. But the web was too closely woven around to admit of my escaping.—Will you, can you believe any thing half so atrocious, as that your father should have called on this same man not only to prove the violent and insubordinate language I had used in reference to the commanding officer in my own rooms, but also to substantiate a charge of cowardice, grounded on the unwillingness I had expressed to accompany the expedition, and the extraordinary trepidation I had evinced, while preparing for the duty, manifested, as it was stated to be, by the various errors he had rectified in my equipment with his own hand? Yes, even this pitiful charge was one of the many preferred; but the severest was that which he had the unblushing effrontery to make the subject of public investigation, rather than of private redress—the blow I had struck him in his own apartments. And who was his witness in this monstrous charge?—your mother, Clara. Yea, I stood as a criminal in her presence; and yet she came forward to tender an evidence that was to consign me to a disgraceful sentence. My vile prosecutor had, moreover, the encouragement, the sanction of his colonel throughout, and by him he was upheld in every contemptible charge his ingenuity could devise. Do you not anticipate the result?—I was found guilty, and dismissed the service.

"How acted my brother officers, when, previously to the trial, I alluded to the damnable treachery of your father? Did they condemn his conduct, or sympathise with me in my misfortune?—No; they shrugged their shoulders, and coldly observed, I ought to have known better than to trust one against whom they had so often cautioned me; but that as I had selected him for my friend, I should have bestowed a whole, and not a half confidence upon him. He had had the hypocrisy to pretend to them he had violated no trust, since he had honourably espoused a lady whom I had introduced to him as a cousin, and in whom I appeared to have no other interest than that of relationship. Not, they said, that they believed he actually did entertain that impression; but still the excuse was too plausible, and had been too well studied by my cunning rival, to be openly refuted. As for the mere fact of his supplanting me, they thought it an excellent thing,—a ruse d'amour for which they never would have given him credit; and although they admitted it was provoking enough to be ousted out of one's mistress in that cool sort of way, still I should not so far have forgotten myself as to have struck him while he was unarmed, when it was so easy to have otherwise fastened an insult on him. Such," bitterly pursued Wacousta, "was the consolation I received from men, who, a few short weeks before, had been sedulous to gain and cultivate my friendship,—but even this was only vouchsafed antecedent to my trial. When the sentence was promulgated, announcing my dismissal from the service, every back was turned upon me, as though I had been found guilty of some dishonourable action or some disgraceful crime; and, on the evening of the same day, when I threw from me for ever an uniform that I now loathed from my inmost soul, there was not one among those who had often banqueted at my expense, who had the humanity to come to me and say, 'Sir Reginald Morton, farewell.'

"What agonies of mind I endured,—what burning tears I nightly shed upon a pillow I was destined to press in freezing loneliness,—what hours of solitude I passed, far from the haunts of my fellow-men, and forming plans of vengeance,—it would take much longer time to relate than I have actually bestowed on my unhappy history. To comprehend their extent and force, you must understand the heart of fire in which the deep sense of injury had taken root; but the night wears away, and briefly told must be the remainder of my tale. The rebellion of forty-five saw me in arms in the Scottish ranks; and, in one instance, opposed to the regiment from which I had been so ignominiously expelled. Never did revenge glow like a living fire in the heart of man as it did in mine; for the effect of my long brooding in solitude had been to inspire me with a detestation, not merely for those who had been most rancorous in their enmity, but for every thing that wore the uniform, from the commanding officer down to the meanest private. Every blow that I dealt, every life that I sacrificed, was an insult washed away from my attainted honour; but him whom I most sought in the melee I never could reach. At length the corps to which I had attached myself was repulsed; and I saw, with rage in my heart, that my enemy still lived to triumph in the fruit of his villainy.

"Although I was grown considerably in stature at this period, and was otherwise greatly altered in appearance, I had been recognised in the action by numbers of the regiment; and, indeed, more than once I had, in the intoxication of my rage, accompanied the blow that slew or maimed one of my former associates with a declaration of the name of him who inflicted it. The consequence was, I was denounced as a rebel and an outlaw, and a price was put upon my head. Accustomed, however, as I had ever been, to rocks and fastnesses, I had no difficulty in eluding the vigilance of those who were sent in pursuit of me; and thus compelled to live wholly apart from my species, I at length learned to hate them, and to know that man is the only enemy of man upon earth.

"A change now came ever the spirit of my vengeance; for about this period your mother died. I had never ceased to love, even while I despised her; and notwithstanding, had she, after her flagrant inconstancy, thrown herself into my arms, I should have rejected her with scorn, still I was sensible no other woman could ever supply her place in my affection. She was, in truth, the only being I had ever looked upon with fondness; and deeply even as I had been injured by her, I wept her memory with many a scalding tear. This, however, only increased my hatred for him who had rioted in her beauty, and supplanted me in her devotedness. I had the means of learning, occasionally, all that passed in the regiment; and the same account that brought me the news of your mother's death also gave me the intelligence that three children had been the fruit of her union with De Haldimar. How," pursued Wacousta, with bitter energy, "shall I express the deep loathing I felt for those children? It seemed to me as if their existence had stamped a seal of infamy on my own brow; and I hated them, even in their childhood, as the offspring of an abhorred, and, as it appeared to me, an unnatural union. I heard, moreover (and this gave me pleasure), that their father doated on them; and from that moment I resolved to turn his cup of joy into bitterness, even as he had turned mine. I no longer sought his life; for the jealousy that had half impelled that thirst existed no longer: but, deeming his cold nature at least accessible through his parental affection, I was resolved that in his children he should suffer a portion of the agonies he had inflicted on me. I waited, however, until they should be grown up to an age when the heart of the parent would be more likely to mourn their loss; and then I was determined my vengeance should be complete.

"Circumstances singularly favoured my design. Many years afterwards, the regiment formed one of the expedition against Quebec under General Wolfe. They were commanded by your father, who, in the course of promotion, had obtained the lieutenant-colonelcy; and I observed by the army list, that a subaltern of the same name, whom I presumed to be his eldest son, was in the corps. Here was a field for my vengeance beyond any I could have hoped for. I contrived to pass over into Cornwall, the ban of outlawry being still unrepealed; and having procured from my brother a sum sufficient for my necessities, and bade him an eternal farewell, embarked in a fishing-boat for the coast of France, whence I subsequently took a passage to this country. At Montreal I found the French general, who gladly received my allegiance as a subject of France, and gave me a commission in one of the provincial corps that usually served in concert with our Indian allies. With the general I soon became a favourite; and, as a mark of his confidence at the attack on Quebec, he entrusted me with the command of a detached irregular force, consisting partly of Canadians and partly of Indians, intended to harass the flanks of the British army. This gave me an opportunity of being at whatever point of the field I might think most favourable to my design; and I was too familiar with the detested uniform of the regiment not to be able to distinguish it from afar. In a word, Clara, for I am weary of my own tale, in that engagement I had an opportunity of recognising your brother. He struck me by his martial appearance as he encouraged his grenadiers to the attack of the French columns; and, as I turned my eye upon him in admiration, I was stung to the soul by his resemblance to his father. Vengeance thrilled throughout every fibre of my frame at that moment. The opportunity I had long sought was at length arrived; and already, in anticipation, I enjoyed the conquest his fall would occasion to my enemy. I rushed within a few feet of my victim; but the bullet aimed at his heart was received in the breast of a faithful soldier, who had flown to intercept it. How I cursed the meddler for his officiousness!"

"Oh, that soldier was your nephew," eagerly interrupted Clara, pointing towards her companion, who had fallen into a profound slumber, "the husband of this unfortunate woman. Frank Halloway (for by that name was he alone known in the regiment) loved my brother as though he had been of the same blood. He it was who flew to receive the ball that was destined for another. But I nursed him on his couch of suffering, and with my own hands prepared his food and dressed his wound. Oh, if pity can touch your heart (and I will not believe that a heart that once felt as you say yours has felt can be inaccessible to pity), let the recollection of your nephew's devotedness to my mother's child disarm you of vengeance, and induce you to restore us!"

"Never!" thundered Wacousta,—"never! The very circumstance you have now named is an additional incentive to my vengeance. My nephew saved the life of your brother at the hazard of his own; and how has he been rewarded for the generous deed? By an ignominious death, inflicted, perhaps, for some offence not more dishonouring than those which have thrown me an outcast upon these wilds; and that at the command and in the presence of the father of him whose life he was fool enough to preserve. Yet, what but ingratitude of the grossest nature could a Morton expect at the hands of the false family of De Haldimar! They were destined to be our bane, and well have they fulfilled the end for which they were created."

"Almighty Providence!" aspirated the sinking Clara, as she turned her streaming eyes to heaven; "can it be that the human heart can undergo such change? Can this be the being who once loved my mother with a purity and tenderness of affection that angels themselves might hallow with approval; or is all that I have heard but a bewildering dream?"

"No, Clara," calmly and even solemnly returned the warrior; "it is no dream, but a reality—a sad, dreadful, heart-rending reality; yet, if I am that altered being, to whom is the change to be ascribed? Who turned the generous current of my blood into a river of overflowing gall? Who, when my cup was mantling with the only bliss I coveted upon earth, traitorously emptied it, and substituted a heart-corroding poison in its stead? Who blighted my fair name, and cast me forth an alien in the land of my forefathers? Who, in a word, cut me off from every joy that existence can impart to man? Who did all this? Your father! But these are idle words. What I have been, you know; what I now am, and through what agency I have been rendered what I now am, you know also. Not more fixed is fate than my purpose. Your brother dies even on the spot on which my nephew died; and you, Clara, shall be my bride; and the first thing your children shall be taught to lisp shall be curses on the vile name of De Haldimar!"

"Once more, in the name of my sainted mother, I implore you to have mercy," shrieked the unhappy Clara. "Oh!" she continued, with vehement supplication, "let the days of your early love be brought back to' your memory, that your heart may be softened; and cut yourself not wholly off from your God, by the commission of such dreadful outrages. Again I conjure you, restore us to my father."

"Never!" savagely repeated Wacousta. "I have passed years of torture in the hope of such an hour as this; and now that fruition is within my grasp, may I perish if I forego it! Ha, sir!" turning from the almost fainting Clara to Sir Everard, who had listened with deep attention to the history of this extraordinary man;—"for this," and he thrust aside the breast of his hunting coat, exhibiting the scar of a long but superficial wound,—"for this do you owe me a severe reckoning. I would recommend you, however,"—and he spoke in mockery,—"when next you drive a weapon into the chest of an unresisting enemy, to be more certain of your aim. Had that been as true as the blow from the butt of your rifle, I should not have lived to triumph in this hour. I little deemed," he pursued, still addressing the nearly heart-broken officer in the same insolent strain, "that my intrigue with that dark-eyed daughter of the old Canadian would have been the means of throwing your companion so speedily into my power, after his first narrow escape. Your disguise was well managed, I confess; and but that there is an instinct about me, enabling me to discover a De Haldimar, as a hound does the deer, by scent, you might have succeeded in passing for what you appeared. But" (and his tone suddenly changed its irony for fierceness) "to the point, sir. That you are the lover of this girl I clearly perceive, and death were preferable to a life embittered by the recollection that she whom we love reposes in the arms of another. No such kindness is meant you, however. To-morrow you shall return to the fort; and, when there, you may tell your colonel, that, in exchange for a certain miniature and letters, which, in the hurry of departure, I dropped in his apartment, some ten days since, Sir Reginald Morton, the outlaw, has taken his daughter Clara to wife, but without the solemnisation of those tedious forms that bound himself in accursed union with her mother. Oh! what would I not give," he continued, bitterly, "to witness the pang inflicted on his false heart, when first the damning truth arrests his ear. Never did I know the triumph of my power until now; for what revenge can be half so sweet as that which attains a loathed enemy through the dishonour of his child? But, hark! what mean those sounds?"

A loud yelling was now heard at some distance in rear of the tent. Presently the bounding of many feet on the turf was distinguishable; and then, at intervals, the peculiar cry that announces the escape of a prisoner. Wacousta started to his feet, and fiercely grasping his tomahawk, advanced to the front of the tent, where he seemed to listen for a moment attentively, as if endeavouring to catch the direction of the pursuit.

"Ha! by Heaven!" he exclaimed, "there must be treachery in this, or yon slippery captain would not so soon be at his flight again, bound as I had bound him." Then uttering a deafening yell, and rushing past Sir Everard, near whom he paused an instant, as if undecided whether he should not first dispose of him, as a precautionary measure, he flew with the speed of an antelope in the direction in which he was guided by the gradually receding sounds.

"The knife, Miss de Haldimar," exclaimed Sir Everard, after a few moments of breathless and intense anxiety. "See, there is one in the belt that Ellen Halloway has girt around her loins. Quick, for Heaven's sake, quick; our only chance of safety is in this."

With an activity arising from her despair, the unhappy Clara sprang from the rude couch on which she had been left by Wacousta, and, stooping over the form of the maniac, extended her hand to remove the weapon from her side; but Ellen, who had been awakened from her long slumber by the yells just uttered, seemed resolute to prevent it. A struggle for its possession now ensued between these frail and delicate beings; in which Clara, however, had the advantage, not only from the recumbent position of her opponent, but from the greater security of her grasp. At length, with a violent effort, she contrived to disengage it from the sheath, around which Ellen had closely clasped both her hands; but, with the quickness of thought, the latter were again clenched round the naked blade, and without any other evident motive than what originated in the obstinacy of her madness, the unfortunate woman fiercely attempted to wrest it away. In the act of doing so, her hands were dreadfully cut; and Clara, shocked at the sight of the blood she had been the means of shedding, lost all the energy she had summoned, and sunk senseless at the feet of the maniac, who now began to utter the most piteous cries.

"Oh, God! we are lost," exclaimed Sir Everard; "the voice of that wretched woman has alarmed our enemy, and even now I hear him approaching. Quick, Clara, give me the knife. But no, it is now too late; he is here."

At that instant, the dark form of a warrior rushed noiselessly to the spot on which he stood. The officer turned his eyes in desperation on his enemy, but a single glance was sufficient to assure him it was not Wacousta. The Indian paused not in his course, but passing close round the tree to which the baronet was attached, made a circular movement, that brought him in a line with the direction that had been taken by his enemy; and again they were left alone.

A new fear now oppressed the heart of the unfortunate Valletort, even to agony: Clara still lay senseless, speechless, before him; and his impression was, that, in the struggle, Ellen Halloway had murdered her. The latter yet continued her cries; and, as she held up her hands, he could see by the fire-light they were covered with blood. An instinctive impulse caused him to bound forward to the assistance of the motionless Clara; when, to his infinite surprise and joy, he discovered the cord, which had bound him to the tree, to be severed. The Indian who had just passed had evidently been his deliverer; and a sudden flash of recollection recalled the figure of the young warrior that had escaped from the schooner and was supposed to have leaped into the canoe of Oucanasta at the moment when Madeline de Haldimar was removed into that of the Canadian.

In a transport of conflicting feelings, Sir Everard now raised the insensible Clara from the ground; and, having satisfied himself she had sustained no serious injury, prepared for a flight which he felt to be desperate, if not altogether hopeless. There was not a moment to be lost, for the cries of the wretched Ellen increased in violence, as she seemed sensible she was about to be left utterly alone; and ever and anon, although afar off, yet evidently drawing nearer, was to be heard the fierce denouncing yell of Wacousta. The spot on which the officer stood, was not far from that whence his unfortunate friend had commenced his flight on the first memorable occasion; and as the moon shone brightly in the cloudless heavens, there could be no mistake in the course he was to pursue. Dashing down the steep, therefore, with all the speed his beloved burden would enable him to attain, he made immediately for the bridge, over which his only chance of safety lay.

It unfortunately happened, however, that, induced either by the malice of her insanity, or really terrified at the loneliness of her position, the wretched Ellen Halloway had likewise quitted the tent, and now followed close in the rear of the fugitives, still uttering the same piercing cries of anguish. The voice of Wacousta was also again heard in the distance; and Sir Everard had the inexpressible horror to find that, guided by the shrieks of the maniac woman, he was now shaping his course, not to the tent where he had left his prisoners, but in an oblique direction towards the bridge; where he evidently hoped to intercept them. Aware of the extreme disadvantages under which he laboured in a competition of speed with his active enemy, the unhappy officer would have here terminated the struggle, had he not been partially sustained by the hope that the detachment prayed for by De Haldimar, through the friendly young chief, to whom he owed his own liberation, might be about this time on its way to attempt their rescue. This thought supported his faltering resolution, although nearly exhausted with his efforts—compelled, as he was, to sustain the motionless form of the slowly reviving Clara; and he again braced himself to the unequal flight The moon still shone beautifully bright, and he could now distinctly see the bridge over which he was to pass; but notwithstanding he strained his eyes as he advanced, no vestige of a British uniform was to be seen in the open space that lay beyond. Once he turned to regard his pursuers. Ellen was a few yards only in his rear; and considerably beyond her rose, in tall relief against the heavens, the gigantic form of the warrior. The pursuit of the latter was now conducted with a silence that terrified even more than the yells he had previously uttered; and he gained so rapidly on his victims, that the tread of his large feet was now distinctly audible. Again the officer, with despair in his heart, made the most incredible exertions to reach the bridge, without seeming to reflect that, even when there, no security was offered him against his enemy. Once, as he drew nearer, he fancied he saw the dark heads of human beings peering from under that part of the arch which had afforded cover to De Haldimar and himself oh the memorable occasion of their departure with the Canadian; and, convinced that the warriors of Wacousta had been sent there to lie in ambuscade and intercept his retreat, his hopes were utterly paralysed; and although he stopped not, his flight was rather mechanical than the fruit of any systematic plan of escape.

He had now gained the extremity of the bridge, with Ellen Halloway and Wacousta close in his rear, when suddenly the heads of many men were once more distinguishable, even in the shadow of the arch that overhung the sands of the river. Three individuals detached themselves from the group and leaping upon the further extremity of the bridge, moved rapidly to meet him. Meanwhile the baronet had stopped suddenly, as if in doubt whether to advance or to recede. His suspense was but momentary. Although the persons of these men were disguised as Indian warriors, the broad moonlight that beamed full on their countenances, disclosed the well-remembered features of Blessington, Erskine, and Charles de Haldimar. The latter sprang before his companions, and, uttering a cry of joy, sank in speechless agony on the neck of his still unconscious sister.

215

"For God's sake, free me, De Haldimar!" exclaimed the excited baronet, disengaging his charge from the embrace of his friend. "This is no moment for congratulation. Erskine, Blessington, see you not who is behind me? Be upon your guard; defend your lives!" And as he spoke, he rushed forward with feint and tottering steps to place his companions between the unhappy girl and the danger that threatened her.

The swords of the officers were drawn; but instead of advancing upon the formidable being, who stood as if paralysed at this unexpected rencontre, the two seniors contented themselves with assuming a defensive attitude,—retiring slowly and gradually towards the other extremity of the bridge.

Overcome by his emotion, Charles de Haldimar had not noticed this action of his companions, and stood apparently riveted to the spot. The voice of Blessington calling on him by name to retire, seemed to arouse the dormant consciousness of the unhappy maniac. She uttered a piercing shriek, and, springing forward, sank on her knees at his feet, exclaiming, as she forcibly detained him by his dress,—

"Almighty Heaven! where am I? surely that was Captain Blessington's kind voice I heard; and you—you are Charles de Haldimar. Oh! save my husband; plead for him with your father!——but no," she continued wildly,—"he is dead—he is murdered! Behold these hands all covered with his blood! Oh!——"

"Ha! another De Haldimar!" exclaimed Wacousta, recovering his slumbering energies, "this spot seems indeed fated for our meeting. More than thrice have I been balked of my just revenge, but now will I secure it. Thus, Ellen, do I avenge your husband's and my nephew's death. My own wrongs demand another sacrifice. But, ha! where is she? where is Clara? where is my bride?"

Bounding over the ill-fated De Haldimar, who lay, even in death, firmly clasped in the embrace of the wretched Ellen, the fierce man dashed furiously forward to renew his pursuit of the fugitives. But suddenly the extremity of the bridge was filled with a column of armed men, that kept issuing from the arch beneath. Sensible of his danger, he sought to make good his retreat; but when he turned for the purpose, the same formidable array met his view at the opposite extremity; and both parties now rapidly advanced in double quick time, evidently with a view of closing upon and taking him prisoner. In this dilemma, his only hope was in the assistance that might be rendered him by his warriors. A yell, so terrific as to be distinctly heard in the fort itself, burst from his vast chest, and rolled in prolonged echoes through the forest. It was faintly answered from the encampment, and met by deep but noiseless curses from the exasperated soldiery, whom the sight of their murdered officer was momentarily working into frenzy.

"Kill him not, for your lives!—I command you, men, kill him not!" muttered Captain Blessington with suppressed passion, as his troops were preparing to immolate him on their clustering bayonets. "Such a death were, indeed, mercy to such a villain."

"Ha! ha!" laughed Wacousta in bitter scorn; "who is there of all your accursed regiment who will dare to take him alive?" Then brandishing his tomahawk around him, to prevent their finally closing, he dealt his blows with such astonishing velocity, that no unguarded point was left about his person; and more than one soldier was brought to the earth in the course of the unequal struggle.

"By G—d!" said Captain Erskine, "are the two best companies of the regiment to be kept at bay by a single desperado? Shame on ye, fellows! If his hands are too many for you, lay him by the heels."

This ruse was practised with success. In attempting to defend himself from the attack of those who sought to throw him down, the warrior necessarily left his upper person exposed; when advantage was taken to close with him and deprive him of the play of his arms. It was not, however, without considerable difficulty, that they succeeded in disarming and binding his hands; after which a strong cord being fastened round his waist, he was tightly lashed to a gun, which, contrary to the original intention of the governor, had been sent out with the expedition. The retreat of the detachment then commenced rapidly; but it was not without being hotly pursued by the band of warriors the yell of Wacousta had summoned in pursuit, that they finally gained the fort: under what feelings of sorrow for the fate of an officer so beloved, we leave it to our readers to imagine.

CHAPTER XII.

The morning of the next day dawned on few who had pressed their customary couches—on none, whose feverish pulse and bloodshot eye failed to attest the utter sleeplessness in which the night had been passed. Numerous groups of men were to be seep assembling after the reveille, in various parts of the barrack square—those who had borne a part in the recent expedition commingling with those who had not, and recounting to the latter, with mournful look and voice, the circumstances connected with the bereavement of their universally lamented officer. As none, however, had seen the blow struck that deprived him of life, although each had heard the frantic exclamations of a voice that had been recognised for Ellen Halloway's, much of the marvellous was necessarily mixed up with truth in their narrative,—some positively affirming Mr. de Haldimar had not once quitted his party, and declaring that nothing short of a supernatural agency could have transported him unnoticed to the fatal spot, where, in their advance, they had beheld him murdered. The singular appearance of Ellen Halloway also, at that moment, on the very bridge on which she had pronounced her curse on the family of De Haldimar, and in company with the terrible and mysterious being who had borne her off in triumph on that occasion to the forest, and under circumstances calculated to excite the most superstitious impressions, was not without its weight in determining their rude speculations; and all concurred in opinion, that the death of the unfortunate young officer was a judgment on their colonel for the little mercy he had extended to the noble-hearted Halloway.

Then followed allusion to their captive, whose gigantic stature and efforts at escape, tremendous even as the latter were, were duly exaggerated by each, with the very laudable view of claiming a proportionate share of credit for his own individual exertions; and many and various were the opinions expressed as to the manner of death he should be made to suffer. Among the most conspicuous of the orators were those with whom our readers have already made slight acquaintance in our account of the sortie by Captain Erskine's company for the recovery of the supposed body of Frederick de Haldimar. One was for impaling him alive, and setting him up to rot on the platform above the gate. Another for blowing him from the muzzle of a twenty-four pounder, into the centre of the first band of Indians that approached the fort, that thus perceiving they had lost the strength and sinew of their cunning war, they might be the more easily induced to propose terms of peace. A third was of opinion he ought to be chained to the top of the flag-staff, as a target, to be shot at with arrows only, contriving never to touch a mortal part. A fourth would have had him tied naked over the sharp spikes that constituted the chevaux-de-frize garnishing the sides of the drawbridge. Each devised some new death—proposed some new torture; but all were of opinion, that simply to be shot, or even to be hanged, was too merciful a punishment for the wretch who had so wantonly and inhumanly butchered the kind-hearted, gentle-mannered officer, whom they had almost all known and loved from his very boyhood; and they looked forward, with mingled anxiety and vengeance, to the moment when, summoned as it was expected he shortly would be, before the assembled garrison, he would be made to expiate the atrocity with his blood.

While the men thus gave indulgence to their indignation and their grief, their officers were even mere painfully affected. The body of the ill-fated Charles had been borne to his apartment, where, divested of its disguise, it had again been inducted in such apparel as was deemed suited to the

221

purpose. Extended on the very bed on which he lay at the moment when she, whose maniac raving, and forcible detention, had been the immediate cause of his destruction, had preferred her wild but fruitless supplication for mercy, he exhibited, even in death, the same delicate beauty that had characterised him on that occasion; yet, with a mildness and serenity of expression on his still, pale features, strongly in contrast with the agitation and glow of excitement that then distinguished him. Never was human loveliness in death so marked as in Charles de Haldimar; and but for the deep wound that, dividing his clustering locks, had entered from the very crown of the head to the opening of his marble brow, one ignorant of his fate might have believed he but profoundly slept. Several women of the regiment were occupied in those offices about the corpse, which women alone are capable of performing at such moments, and as they did so, suffered their tears to flow silently yet abundantly over him, who was no longer sensible either of human grief or of human joy. Close at the head of the bed stood an old man, with his face buried in his hands; the latter reposing against the wainscoting of the room. He, too, wept, but his weeping was more audible, more painful, and accompanied by suffocating sobs. It was the humble, yet almost paternally attached servant of the defunct—the veteran Morrison.

Around the bed were grouped nearly all the officers, standing in attitudes indicative of anxiety and interest, and gazing mournfully on the placid features of their ill-fated friend. All, on entering, moved noiselessly over the rude floor, as though fearful of disturbing the repose of one who merely slumbered; and the same precaution was extended to the brief but heartfelt expressions of sorrow that passed, from one to the other, as they gazed on all that remained of the gentle De Haldimar. At length the preparations of the women having been completed, they retired from the room, leaving one of their number only, rather out of respect than necessity, to remain by the corpse. When they were departed, this woman, the wife of one of Blessington's sergeants, and the same who had been present at the scene between Ellen Halloway and the deceased, cut off a large lock of his beautiful hair, and separating it into small tresses, handed one to each of the officers. This considerate action, although unsolicited on the part of the latter, deeply touched them, as indicating a sense of the high estimation in which the youth bad been held. It was a tribute to the memory of him they mourned, of the purest kind; and each, as he received his portion, acknowledged with a mournful but approving look, or nod, or word, the motive that bad prompted the offering. Nor was it a source of less satisfaction, melancholy even as that satisfaction was, to perceive that, after having set aside another lock, probably for the sister of the deceased, she selected and consigned to the bosom of her dress a third, evidently intended for herself. The whole scene was in striking contrast with the almost utter absence of all preparation or concern that had preceded the interment of Murphy, on a former occasion. In one, the rude soldier was mourned,—in the other, the gentle friend was lamented; nor the latter alone by the companions to whom intimacy had endeared him, but by those humbler dependants, who knew him only through those amiable attributes of character, which were ever equally extended to all. Gradually the officers now moved away in the same noiseless manner in which they had approached, either in pursuance of their several duties, or to make their toilet of the morning. Two only of their number remained near the couch of death.

"Poor unfortunate De Haldimar!" observed one of these, in a low tone, as if speaking to himself; "too fatally, indeed, have your forebodings been realised; and what I considered as the mere despondency of a mind crashed into feebleness by an accumulation of suffering, was, after all, but the first presentiment of a death no human power might avert. By Heaven! I would give up half my own being to be able to reanimate that form once more,—but the wish is vain."

"Who shall announce the intelligence to his sister?" sighed his companion. "Never will that already nearly heart-broken girl be able to survive the shock of her brother's death. Blessington, you alone are fitted to such a task; and, painful as it is, you must undertake it. Is the colonel apprised of the dreadful truth, do you know?"

"He is. It was told him at the moment of our arrival last night; but from the little outward emotion displayed by him, I should be tempted to infer he had almost anticipated some such catastrophe."

"Poor, poor Charles!" bitterly exclaimed Sir Everard Valletort—for it was he. "What would I not give to recall the rude manner in which I spurned you from me last night. But, alas! what could I do, laden with such a trust, and pursued, without the power of defence, by such an enemy? Little, indeed, did I imagine what was so speedily to be your doom! Blessington," he pursued, with increased emotion, "it grieves me to wretchedness to think that he, whom I loved as though he had been my twin brother, should have perished with his last thoughts, perhaps, lingering on the seeming unkindness with which I had greeted him after so anxious an absence."

"Nay, if there be blame, it must attach to me," sorrowfully observed Captain Blessington. "Had Erskine and myself not retired before the savage, as we did, our unfortunate friend would in all probability have been alive at this very hour. But in our anxiety to draw the former into the ambuscade we had prepared for him, we utterly overlooked that Charles was not retreating with us."

"How happened it," demanded Sir Everard, his attention naturally directed to the subject by the preceding remarks, "that you lay thus in ambuscade, when the object of the expedition, as solicited by Frederick de Haldimar, was an attempt to reach us in the encampment of the Indians?"

"It certainly was under that impression we left the fort; but, on coming to the spot where the friendly Indian lay waiting to conduct us, he proposed the plan we subsequently adopted as the most likely, not only to secure the escape of the prisoners, whom he pledged himself to liberate, but to defend ourselves with advantage against Wacousta and the immediate guard set over them, should they follow in pursuit. Erskine approving, as well as myself, of the plan, we halted at the bridge, and disposed of our men under each extremity; so that, if attacked by the Indians in front, we might be enabled to throw them into confusion by taking them in rear, as they flung themselves upon the bridge. The event seemed to answer our expectations. The alarm raised in the encampment satisfied us the young Indian had contrived to fulfil his promise; and we momentarily looked for the appearance of those whose flight we naturally supposed would be directed towards the bridge. To our great surprise, however, we remarked that the sounds of pursuit, instead of approaching us, seemed to take an opposite direction, apparently towards the point whence we had seen the prisoners disembarked in the morning. At length, when almost tempted to regret we had not pushed boldly on, in conformity with our first intention, we heard the shrill cries of a woman; and, not long afterwards, the sounds of human feet rushing down the slope. What our sensations were, you may imagine; for we all believed it to be either Clara or Madeline de Haldimar fleeing alone, and pursued by our ferocious enemies. To show ourselves would, we were sensible, be to ensure the death of the pursued, before we could possibly come up; and, although it was with difficulty we repressed the desire to rush forward to the rescue, our better judgment prevailed. Finally we saw you approach, followed closely by what appeared to be a mere boy of an Indian, and, at a considerable distance, by the tall warrior of the Fleur de lis. We imagined there was time enough for you to gain the bridge; and finding your more formidable pursuer was only accompanied by the youth already alluded to, conceived at that moment the design of making him our prisoner. Still there were half a dozen muskets ready to be levelled on him should he approach too near to his fugitives, or manifest any other design than that of simply recapturing them. How well our plan succeeded you are aware; but, alas!" and he glanced sorrowfully at the corpse, "why was our success to be embittered by so great a sacrifice?"

"Ah, would to Heaven that he at least had been spared," sighed Sir Everard, as he took the wan white hand of his friend in his own; "and yet I know not: he looks so calm, so happy in death, it is almost selfish to repine he has escaped the horrors that still await us in this dreadful warfare. But what of Frederick and Madeline de Haldimar? From the statement you have given, they must have been liberated by the young Ottawa before he came to me; yet, what could have induced them to have taken a course of flight so opposite to that which promised their only chance of safety?"

"Heaven only knows," returned Captain Blessington. "I fear they have again been recaptured by the savages; in which case their doom is scarcely doubtful; unless, indeed, our prisoner of last night be given up in exchange for them."

"Then will their liberty be purchased at a terrible price," remarked the baronet. "Will you believe, Blessington, that that man, whose enmity to our colonel seems almost devilish, was once an officer in this very regiment?"

"You astonish me, Valletort.—Impossible! and yet it has always been apparent to me they were once associates."

"I heard him relate his history only last night to Clara, whom he had the audacity to sully with proposals to become his bride," pursued the baronet. "His tale was a most extraordinary one. He narrated it, however, only up to the period when the life of De Haldimar was attempted by him at Quebec. But with his subsequent history we are all acquainted, through the fame of his bloody atrocities in all the posts that have fallen into the hands of Ponteac. That man, savage and even fiendish as he now is, was once possessed of the noblest qualities. I am sorry to say it; but Colonel de Haldimar has brought this present affliction upon himself. At some future period I will tell you all."

"Alas!" said Captain Blessington, "poor Charles, then, has been made to pay the penalty of his father's errors; and, certainly, the greatest of these was his dooming the unfortunate Halloway to death in the manner he did."

"What think you of the fact of Halloway being the nephew of this extraordinary man, and both of high family?" demanded Sir Everard.

"Indeed! and was the latter, then, aware of the connection?"

"Not until last night," replied Sir Everard. "Some observations made by the wretched wife of Halloway, in the course of which she named his true name, (which was that of the warrior also,) first indicated the fact to the latter. But, what became of that unfortunate creature?—was she brought in?"

"I understand not," said Captain Blessington. "In the confusion and hurry of securing our prisoner, and the apprehension of immediate attack from his warriors, Ellen was entirely overlooked. Some of my men say they left her lying, insensible, on the spot whence they had raised the body of our unfortunate friend, which they had some difficulty in releasing from her convulsive embrace. But, hark! there is the first drum for parade, and I have not yet exchanged my Indian garb."

Captain Blessington now quitted the room, and Sir Everard, relieved from the restraining presence of his companions, gave free vent to his emotion, throwing himself upon the body of his friend, and giving utterance to the feelings of anguish that oppressed his heart.

He had continued some minutes in this position, when he fancied he felt the warm tears of a human being bedewing a hand that reposed on the neck of his unfortunate friend. He looked up, and, to his infinite surprise, beheld Clara de Haldimar standing before him at the opposite side of the bed. Her likeness to her brother, at that moment, was so striking, that, for a second or two, the irrepressible thought passed through the mind of the officer, it was not a living being he gazed upon, but the immaterial spirit of his friend. The whole attitude and appearance of the wretched girl, independently of the fact of her noiseless entrance, tended to favour the delusion. Her features, of an ashy paleness, seemed fixed, even as those of the corpse beneath him; and, but for the tears that coursed silently down her cheek, there was scarcely an outward evidence of emotion. Her dress was

230

a simple white robe, fastened round her waist with a pale blue riband; and over her shoulders hung her redundant hair, resembling in colour, and disposed much in the manner of that of her brother, which had been drawn negligently down to conceal the wound on his brow. For some moments the baronet gazed at her in speechless agony. Her tranquil exterior was torture to him; for he, feared it betokened some alienation of reason. He would have preferred to witness the most hysteric convulsion of grief, rather than that traitorous calm; and yet he had not the power to seek to remove it.

"You are surprised to see me here, mingling my grief with yours, Sir Everard," she at length observed, with the same calm mien, and in tones of touching sweetness. "I came, with my father's permission, to take a last farewell of him whose death has broken my heart. I expected to be alone; but—Nay, do not go," she added, perceiving that the officer was about to depart. "Had you not been here, I should have sent for you; for we have both a sacred duty to perform. May I not ask your hand?"

More and more dismayed at her collected manner, the young officer gazed at her with the deepest sorrow depicted in every line of his own countenance. He extended his hand, and Clara, to his surprise, grasped and pressed it firmly.

"It was the wish of this poor boy that his Clara should be the wife of his friend, Sir Everard. Did he ever express such to you?"

"It was the fondest desire of his heart," returned the baronet, unable to restrain the emotion of joy that mingled, despite of himself, with his worst apprehensions.

"I need not ask how you received his proposal," continued Clara, with the same calmness of manner. "Last night," she pursued solemnly, "I was the bride of the murderer of my brother, of the lover of my mother,—tomorrow night I may be the bride of death; but to-night I am the bride of my brother's friend. Yes, here am I come to pledge myself to the fulfilment of his wish. If you deem a heart-broken girl not unworthy of you, I am your wife, Sir Everard; and, recollect, it is a solemn pledge, that which a sister gives over the lifeless body of a brother, beloved as this has been."

"Oh, Clara—dearest Clara," passionately exclaimed the excited young man, "if a life devoted to your happiness can repay you for this, count upon it as you would upon your eternal salvation. In you will I love both my friend and the sister he has bequeathed to me. Clara, my betrothed wife, summon all the energies of your nature to sustain this cruel shock; and exert yourself for him who will be to you both a brother and a husband."

As he spoke he drew the unresisting girl towards him, and, locking her in his embrace, pressed, for the first time, the lips, which it had maddened him the preceding night to see polluted by the forcible kisses of Wacousta. But Clara shared not, but merely suffered his momentary happiness. Her cheek wore not the crimson of excitement, neither were her tears discontinued. She seemed as one who mechanically submitted to what she had no power of resistance to oppose; and even in the embrace of her affianced husband, she exhibited the same deathlike calm that had startled him at her first appearance. Religion could not hallow a purer feeling than that which had impelled the action of the young officer. The very consciousness of the sacred pledge having been exchanged over the corpse of his friend, imparted a holiness of fervour to his mind; and even while he pressed her, whom he secretly swore to love with all the affection of a fond brother and a husband united, he felt that if the spirit of him, who slept unconscious of the scene, were suffered to linger near, it would be to hallow it with approval.

"And now," said Clara at length, yet without attempting to disengage herself,—"now that we are united, I would be alone with my brother. My husband, leave me."

Deeply touched at the name of husband, Sir Everard could not refrain from imprinting another kiss on the lips that uttered it. He then gently disengaged himself from his lovely but suffering charge, whom he deposited with her head resting on the bed; and making a significant motion of his hand to the woman, who, as well as old Morrison, had been spectators of the whole scene, stole gently from the apartment, under what mingled emotions of joy and grief it would be difficult to describe.

CHAPTER XIII.

It was the eighth hour of morning, and both officers and men, quitting their ill-relished meal, were to be seen issuing to the parade, where the monotonous roll of the assemblee now summoned them. Presently the garrison was formed in the order we have described in our first volume; that is to say, presenting three equal sides of a square. The vacant space fronted the guard-house, near one extremity of which was to be seen a flight of steps communicating with the rampart, where the flag-staff was erected. Several men were employed at this staff, passing strong ropes through iron pulleys that were suspended from the extreme top, while in the basement of the staff itself, to a height of about twenty feet, were stuck at intervals strong wooden pegs, serving as steps to the artillerymen for greater facility in clearing, when foul, the lines to which the colours were attached. The latter had been removed; and, from the substitution of a cord considerably stronger than that which usually appeared there, it seemed as if some far heavier weight was about to be appended to it. Gradually the men, having completed their unusual preparations, quitted the rampart, and the flagstaff, which was of tapering pine, was left totally unguarded.

The "Attention!" of Major Blackwater to the troops, who had been hitherto standing in attitudes of expectancy that rendered the injunction almost superfluous, announced the approach of the governor. Soon afterwards that officer entered the area, wearing his characteristic dignity of manner, yet exhibiting every evidence of one who had suffered deeply. Preparation for a drum-head court-martial, as in the first case of Halloway, had already been made within the square, and the only actor wanting in the drama was he who was to be tried.

Once Colonel de Haldimar made an effort to command his appearance, but the huskiness of his voice choked his utterance, and he was compelled to pause. After the lapse of a few moments, he again ordered, but in a voice that was remarked to falter,—

"Mr. Lawson, let the prisoner be brought forth."

The feeling of suspense that ensued between the delivery and execution of this command was painful throughout the ranks. All were penetrated with curiosity to behold a man who had several times appeared to them under the most appalling circumstances, and against whom the strongest feeling of indignation had been excited for his barbarous murder of Charles de Haldimar. It was with mingled awe and anger they now awaited his approach. At length the captive was seen advancing from the cell in which he had been confined, his gigantic form towering far above those of the guard of grenadiers by whom he was surrounded; and with a haughtiness in his air, and insolence in his manner, that told he came to confront his enemy with a spirit unsubdued by the fate that too probably awaited him.

Many an eye was turned upon the governor at that moment. He was evidently struggling for composure to meet the scene he felt it to be impossible to avoid; and he turned pale and paler as his enemy drew near.

At length the prisoner stood nearly in the same spot where his unfortunate nephew had lingered on a former occasion. He was unchained; but his hands were firmly secured behind his back. He threw himself into an attitude of carelessness, resting on one foot, and tapping the earth with the other; riveting his eye, at the same time, with an expression of the most daring insolence, on the governor, while his swarthy cheek was moreover lighted up with a smile of the deepest scorn.

"You are Reginald Morton the outlaw, I believe," at length observed the governor in an uncertain tone, that, however, acquired greater firmness as he proceeded,—"one whose life has already been forfeited through his treasonable practices in Europe, and who has, moreover, incurred the penalty of an ignominious death, by acting in this country as a spy of the enemies of England. What say you, Reginald Morton, that you should not be convicted in the death that awaits the traitor?"

"Ha! ha! by Heaven, such cold, pompous insolence amuses me," vociferated Wacousta. "It reminds me of Ensign de Haldimar of nearly five and twenty years back, who was then as cunning a dissembler as he is now." Suddenly changing his ribald tone to one of scorn and rage:—"You BELIEVE me, you say, to be Reginald Morton the outlaw. Well do you know it. I am that Sir Reginald Morton, who became an outlaw, not through his own crimes, but through your villainy. Ay, frown as you may, I heed it not. You may award me death, but shall not chain my tongue. To your whole regiment do I proclaim you for a false, remorseless villain." Then turning his flashing eye along the ranks:—"I was once an officer in this corps, and long before any of you wore the accursed uniform. That man, that fiend, affected to be my friend; and under the guise of friendship, stole into the heart I loved better than my own life. Yes," fervently pursued the excited prisoner, stamping violently with his foot upon the earth, "he robbed me of my affianced wife; and for that I resented an outrage that should have banished him to some

237

lone region, where he might never again pollute human nature with his presence—he caused me to be tried by a court-martial, and dismissed the service. Then, indeed, I became the outlaw he has described, but not until then. Now, Colonel de Haldimar, that I have proclaimed your infamy, poor and inefficient as the triumph be, do your worst—I ask no mercy. Yesterday I thought that years of toilsome pursuit of the means of vengeance were about to be crowned with success; but fate has turned the tables on me and I yield."

To all but the baronet and Captain Blessington this declaration was productive of the utmost surprise. Every eye was turned upon the colonel. He grew impatient under the scrutiny, and demanded if the court, who meanwhile had been deliberating, satisfied of the guilt of the prisoner, had come to a decision in regard to his punishment. An affirmative answer was given, and Colonel de Haldimar proceeded.

"Reginald Morton, with the private misfortunes of your former life we have nothing to do. It is the decision of this court, who are merely met out of form, that you suffer immediate death by hanging, as a just recompense for your double treason to your country. There," and he pointed to the flag-staff, "will you be exhibited to the misguided people whom your wicked artifices have stirred up into hostility against us. When they behold your fate, they will take warning from your example; and, finding we have heads and arms not to suffer offence with impunity, be more readily brought to obedience."

"I understand your allusion," coolly rejoined Wacousta, glancing earnestly at, and apparently measuring with his eye, the dimensions of the conspicuous scaffold on which he was to suffer. "You had ever a calculating head, De Haldimar, where any secret villainy, any thing to promote your own selfish ends, was to be gained by it; but your calculation seems now, methinks, at fault."

Colonel de Haldimar looked at him enquiringly.

"You have STILL a son left," pursued the prisoner with the same recklessness of manner, and in a tone denoting allusion to him who was no more, that caused an universal shudder throughout the ranks. "He is in the hands of the Ottawa Indians, and I am the friend of their great chief, inferior only in power among the tribe to himself. Think you that he will see me hanged up like a dog, and fail to avenge my disgraceful death?"

"Ha! presumptuous renegade, is this the deep game you have in view? Hope you then to stipulate for the preservation of a life every way forfeited to the offended justice of your country? Dare you to cherish the belief, that, after the horrible threats so often denounced by you, you will again be let loose upon a career of crime and blood?"

239

"None of your cant, de Haldimar, as I once observed to you before," coolly retorted Wacousta, with bitter sarcasm. "Consult your own heart, and ask if its catalogue of crime be not far greater than my own: yet I ask not my life. I would but have the manner of my fate altered, and fain would die the death of the soldier I WAS before you rendered me the wretch I AM. Methinks the boon is not so great, if the restoration of your son be the price."

"Do you mean, then," eagerly returned the governor, "that if the mere mode of your death be changed, my son shall be restored?"

"I do," was the calm reply.

"What pledge have we of the fact? What faith can we repose in the word of a fiend, whose brutal vengeance has already sacrificed the gentlest life that ever animated human clay?" Here the emotion of the governor almost choked, his utterance, and considerable agitation and murmuring were manifested in the ranks.

"Gentle, said you?" replied the prisoner, musingly; "then did he resemble his mother, whom I loved, even as his brother resembles you whom I have had so much reason to hate. Had I known the boy to be what you describe, I might have felt some touch of pity even while I delayed not to strike his death blow; but the false moonlight deceived me, and the detested name of De Haldimar, pronounced by the lips of my nephew's wife—that wife whom your cold-blooded severity had widowed and driven mad—was in itself sufficient to ensure his doom."

"Inhuman ruffian!" exclaimed the governor, with increasing indignation; "to the point. What pledge have you to offer that my son will be restored?"

"Nay, the pledge is easily given, and without much risk. You have only to defer my death until your messenger return from his interview with Ponteac. If Captain de Haldimar accompany him back, shoot me as I have requested; if he come not, then it is but to hang me after all."

"Ha! I understand you; this is but a pretext to gain time, a device to enable your subtle brain to plan some mode of escape."

"As you will, Colonel de Haldimar," calmly retorted Wacousta; and again he sank into silence, with the air of one utterly indifferent to results.

"Do you mean," resumed the colonel, "that a request from yourself to the Ottawa chief will obtain the liberation of my son?"

"Unless the Indian be false as yourself, I do."

"And of the lady who is with him?" continued the colonel, colouring with anger.

"Of both."

"How is the message to be conveyed?"

"Ha, sir!" returned the prisoner, drawing himself up to his full height, "now are you arrived at a point that is pertinent. My wampum belt will be the passport, and the safeguard of him you send; then for the communication. There are certain figures, as you are aware, that, traced on bark, answer the same purpose among the Indians with the European language of letters. Let my hands be cast loose," he pursued, but in a tone in which agitation and excitement might be detected, "and if bark be brought me, and a burnt stick or coal, I will give you not only a sample of Indian ingenuity, but a specimen of my own progress in Indian acquirements."

"What, free your hands, and thus afford you a chance of escape?" observed the governor, doubtingly.

Wacousta bent his stedfast gaze on him for a few moments, as if he questioned he had heard aright. Then bursting into a wild and scornful laugh,—"By Heaven!" he exclaimed, "this is, indeed, a high compliment you pay me at the expense of these fine fellows. What, Colonel de Haldimar afraid to liberate an unarmed prisoner, hemmed in by a forest of bayonets? This is good; gentlemen," and he bent himself in sarcastic reverence to the astonished troops, "I beg to offer you my very best congratulations on the high estimation in which you are held by your colonel."

"Peace, sirrah!" exclaimed the governor, enraged beyond measure at the insolence of him who thus held him up to contempt before his men, "or, by Heaven, I will have your tongue cut out!—Mr. Lawson, let what this fellow requires be procured immediately." Then addressing Lieutenant Boyce, who commanded the immediate guard over the prisoner,—"Let his hands be liberated, sir, and enjoin your men to be watchful of the movements of this supple traitor. His activity I know of old to be great, and he seems to have doubled it since he assumed that garb."

The command was executed, and the prisoner stood, once more, free and unfettered in every muscular limb. A deep and unbroken silence ensued; and the return of the adjutant was momentarily expected. Suddenly a loud scream was heard, and the slight figure of a female, clad in white, came rushing from the piazza in which the apartment of the deceased De Haldimar was situated. It was Clara. The guard of Wacousta formed the fourth front of the square; but they were drawn up somewhat in the distance, so as to leave an open space of several feet at the angles. Through one of these the excited girl now passed into the area, with a wildness in her air and appearance that riveted every eye in painful interest upon her. She paused not until she had gained the side of the captive, at whose feet she now sank in an attitude expressive of the most profound despair.

"Tiger!—monster!" she raved, "restore my brother!—give me back the gentle life you have taken, or destroy my own! See, I am a weak defenceless girl: can you not strike?—you who have no pity for the innocent. But come," she pursued, mournfully, regaining her feet and grasping his iron hand,— "come and see the sweet calm face of him you have slain:— come with me, and behold the image of Clara Beverley; and, if you ever loved her as you say you did, let your soul be touched with remorse for your crime."

The excitement and confusion produced by this unexpected interruption was great. Murmurs of compassion for the unhappy Clara, and of indignation against the prisoner, were no longer sought to be repressed by the men; while the officers, quitting their places in the ranks, grouped themselves indiscriminately in the foreground. One, more impatient than his companions, sprang forward, and forcibly drew away the delicate, hand that still grasped that of the captive. It was Sir Everard Valletort.

"Clara, my beloved wife!" he exclaimed, to the astonishment of all who heard him, "pollute not your lips by further communion with such a wretch; his heart is as inaccessible to pity as the rugged rocks on which his spring-life was passed. For Heaven's sake,—for my sake,—linger not within his reach. There is death in his very presence."

"Your wife, sir!" haughtily observed the governor, with irrepressible astonishment and indignation in his voice; "what mean you?—Gentlemen, resume your places in the ranks.—Clara—Miss de Haldimar, I command you to retire instantly to your apartment.—We will discourse of this later, Sir Everard Valletort. I trust you have not dared to offer an indignity to my child."

While he was yet turned to that officer, who had taken his post, as commanded, in the inner angle of the square, and with a countenance that denoted the conflicting emotions of his soul, he was suddenly startled by the confused shout and rushing forward of the whole body, both of officers and men. Before he had time to turn, a loud and well-remembered yell burst upon his ear. The next moment, to his infinite surprise and horror, he beheld the bold warrior rapidly ascending the very staff that had been destined for his scaffold, and with Clara in his arms.

Great was the confusion that ensued. To rush forward and surround the flag-staff, was the immediate action of the troops. Many of the men raised their muskets, and in the excitement of the moment, would have fired, had they not been restrained by their officers, who pointed out the certain destruction it would entail on the unfortunate Clara. With the rapidity of thought, Wacousta had snatched up his victim, while the attention of the troops was directed to the singular conversation passing between the governor and Sir

Everard Valletort, and darting through one of the open angles already alluded to, had gained the rampart before they had recovered from the stupor produced by his daring action. Stepping lightly upon the pegs, he had rapidly ascended to the utmost height of these, before any one thought of following him; and then grasping in his teeth the cord which was to have served for his execution, and holding Clara firmly against his chest, while he embraced the smooth staff with knees and feet closely compressed around it, accomplished the difficult ascent with an ease that astonished all who beheld him. Gradually, as he approached the top, the tapering pine waved to and fro; and at each moment it was expected, that, yielding to their united weight, it would snap asunder, and precipitate both Clara and himself, either upon the rampart, or into the ditch beyond.

More than one officer now attempted to follow the fugitive in his adventurous course; but even Lieutenant Johnstone, the most active and experienced in climbing of the party, was unable to rise more than a few yards above the pegs that afforded a footing, add the enterprise was abandoned as an impossibility. At length Wacousta was seen to gain the extreme summit. For a moment he turned his gaze anxiously beyond the town, in the direction of the bridge; and, after pealing forth one of his terrific yells, exclaimed, exultingly, as he turned his eye upon his enemy:—

"Well, colonel, what think you of this sample of Indian ingenuity? Did I not tell you," he continued, in mockery, "that, if my hands were but free, I would give you a specimen of my progress in Indian acquirements?"

"If you would avoid a death even more terrible than that of hanging," shouted the governor, in a voice of mingled rage and terror, "restore my daughter."

"Ha! ha! ha!—excellent!" vociferated the savage. "You threaten largely, my good governor; but your threats are harmless as those of a weak besieging army before an impregnable fortress. It is for the strongest, however, to propose his terms.—If I restore this girl to life, will you pledge yourself to mine?"

"Never!" thundered Colonel de Haldimar, with unusual energy.—"Men, procure axes; cut the flag-staff down, since this is the only means left of securing yon insolent traitor! Quick to your work: and mark, who first seizes him shall have promotion on the spot."

Axes were instantly procured, and two of the men now lent themselves vigorously to the task. Wacousta seemed to watch these preparations with evident anxiety; and to all it appeared as if his courage had been paralysed by this unexpected action. No sooner, however, had the axemen reached the heart of the staff, than, holding Clara forth over the edge of the rampart, he shouted,—

247

"One stroke more, and she perishes!"

Instantaneously the work was discontinued. A silence of a few moments ensued. Every eye was turned upward,—every heart beat with terror to see the delicate girl, held by a single arm, and apparently about to be precipitated from that dizzying height. Again Wacousta shouted,—

"Life for life, De Haldimar! If I yield her shall I live?"

"No terms shall be dictated to me by a rebel, in the heart of my own fort," returned the governor. "Restore my child, and we will then consider what mercy may be extended to you."

"Well do I know what mercy dwells in such a heart as yours," gloomily remarked the prisoner; "but I come."

"Surround the staff, men," ordered the governor, in a low tone. "The instant he descends, secure him: lash him in every limb, nor suffer even his insolent tongue to be longer at liberty."

"Boyce, for God's sake open the gate, and place men in readiness to lower the drawbridge," implored Sir Everard of the officer of the guard, and in a tone of deep emotion that was not meant to be overheard by the governor. "I fear the boldness of this vengeful man may lead him to some desperate means of escape."

While the officer whom he addressed issued a command, the responsibility of which he fancied he might, under the peculiar circumstances of the moment, take upon himself, Wacousta began his descent, not as before, by adhering to the staff, but by the rope which he held in his left hand, while he still supported the apparently senseless Clara against his right chest with the other.

"Now, Colonel de Haldimar, I hope your heart is at rest," he shouted, as he rapidly glided by the cord; "enjoy your triumph as best may suit your pleasure."

Every eye followed his movement with interest; every heart beat lighter at the certainty of Clara being again restored, and without other injury than the terror she must have experienced in such a scene. Each congratulated himself on the favourable termination of the terrible adventure, yet were all ready to spring upon and secure the desperate author of the wrong. Wacousta had now reached the centre of the flag-staff. Pausing for a moment, he grappled it with his strong and nervous feet, on which he apparently rested, to give a momentary relief to the muscles of his left arm. He then abruptly abandoned his hold, swinging himself out a few yards from the staff, and returning again, dashed his feet against it with a force that caused the weakened mass to vibrate to its very foundation. Impelled by his weight, and the violence of his action, the creaking pine gave way; its lofty top gradually bending over the exterior rampart until it finally snapped asunder, and fell with a loud crash across the ditch.

"Open the gate, down with the drawbridge!" exclaimed the excited governor.

"Down with the drawbridge," repeated Sir Everard to the men already stationed there ready to let loose at the first order. The heavy chains rattled sullenly through the rusty pulleys, and to each the bridge seemed an hour descending. Before it had reached its level, it was covered with the weight of many armed men rushing confusedly to the front; and the foremost of these leaped to the earth before it had sunk into its customary bed. Sir Everard Valletort and Lieutenant Johnstone were in the front, both armed with their rifles, which had been brought them before Wacousta commenced his descent. Without order or combination, Erskine, Blessington, and nearly half of their respective companies, followed as they could; and dispersing as they advanced, sought only which could outstep his fellows in the pursuit.

Meanwhile the fugitive, assisted in his fall by the gradual rending asunder of the staff, had obeyed the impulsion first given to his active form, until, suddenly checking himself by the rope, he dropped with his feet downward into the centre of the ditch. For a moment he disappeared, then came again uninjured to the surface; and in the face of more than fifty men, who, lining the rampart with their muskets levelled to take him at advantage the instant he should reappear, seemed to laugh their efforts to scorn. Holding Clara before him as a shield, through which the bullets of his enemies must pass before they could attain him, he impelled his gigantic form with a backward movement towards the opposite bank, which he rapidly ascended; and, still fronting his enemies, commenced his flight in that manner with a speed which (considering the additional weight of the drenched garments of both) was inconceivable. The course taken by him was not through the town, but circuitously across the common until he arrived on that immediate line whence, as we have before stated, the bridge was distinctly visible from the rampart; on which, nearly the whole of the remaining troops, in defiance of the presence of their austere chief, were now eagerly assembled, watching, with unspeakable interest, the progress of the chase.

Desperate as were the exertions of Wacousta, who evidently continued this mode of flight from a conviction that the instant his person was left exposed the fire-arms of his pursuers would be brought to bear upon him, the two officers in front, animated by the most extraordinary exertions, were rapidly gaining upon him. Already was one within fifty yards of him, when a loud yell was heard from the bridge. This was fiercely answered by the fleeing man, and in a manner that implied his glad sense of coming rescue. In the wild exultation of the moment, he raised Clara high above his head, to show her in triumph to the governor, whose person his keen eye could easily distinguish among those crowded upon the rampart. In the gratified vengeance of that hour, he seemed utterly to overlook the actions of those who were so near him. During this brief scene, Sir Everard had dropped upon one knee, and supporting his elbow on the other, aimed his rifle at the heart of the ravisher of his wife. An exulting shout burst from the pursuing troops. Wacousta bounded a few feet in air, and placing his hand to his side, uttered another yell, more appalling than any that had hitherto escaped him. His flight was now uncertain and wavering. He staggered as one who had received a mortal wound; and discontinuing his unequal mode of retreat, turned his back upon his pursuers, and threw all his remaining energies into a final effort at escape.

Inspirited by the success of his shot, and expecting momentarily to see him fall weakened with the loss of blood, the excited Valletort redoubled his exertions. To his infinite joy, he found that the efforts of the fugitive became feebler at each moment Johnstone was about twenty paces behind him, and the pursuing party at about the same distance from Johnstone. The baronet had now reached his enemy, and already was the butt of his rifle raised with both hands with murderous intent, when suddenly Wacousta, every feature distorted with rage and pain, turned like a wounded lion at bay, and eluding the blow, deposited the unconscious form of his victim upon the sward. Springing upon his infinitely weaker pursuer, he grappled him furiously by the throat, exclaiming through his clenched teeth:—

"Nay then, since you will provoke your fate—be it so. Die like a dog, and be d—d, for having balked me—of my just revenge!"

As he spoke, he hurled the gasping officer to the earth with a violence that betrayed the dreadful excitement of his soul, and again hastened to assure himself of his prize.

Meanwhile, Lieutenant Johnstone had come up, and, seeing his companion struggling as he presumed, with advantage, with his severely wounded enemy, made it his first care to secure the unhappy girl; for whose recovery the pursuit had been principally instituted. Quitting his rifle, he now essayed to raise her in his arms. She was without life or consciousness, and the impression on his mind was that she was dead.

While in the act of raising her, the terrible Wacousta stood at his side, his vast chest heaving forth a laugh of mingled rage and contempt. Before the officer could extricate, with a view of defending himself, his arms were pinioned as though in a vice; and ere he could recover from his surprise, he felt himself lifted up and thrown to a considerable distance.

When he opened his eyes a moment afterwards, he was lying amid the moving feet of his own men.

From the instant of the closing of the unfortunate Valletort with his enemy, the Indians, hastening to the assistance of their chief, had come up, and a desultory fire had already commenced, diverting, in a great degree, the attention of the troops from the pursued. Emboldened by this new aspect of things Wacousta now deliberately grasped the rifle that had been abandoned by Johnstone; and raising it to his shoulder, fired among the group collected on the ramparts. For a moment he watched the result of his shot, and then, pealing forth another fierce yell, he hurled the now useless weapon into the very heart of his pursuers; and again raising Clara in his arms, once more commenced his retreat, which, under cover of the fire of his party, was easily effected.

"Who has fallen?" demanded the governor of his adjutant, perceiving that some one had been hit at his side, yet without taking his eyes off his terrible enemy.

"Mr. Delme, sir," was the reply. "He has been shot through the heart, and his men are bearing him from the rampart."

"This must not be," resumed the governor with energy. "Private feelings must no longer be studied at the expense of the public good. That pursuit is hopeless; and already too many of my officers have fallen. Desire the retreat to be sounded, Mr. Lawson. Captain Wentworth, let one or two covering guns be brought to bear upon the savages. They are gradually increasing hi numbers; and if we delay, the party will be wholly cut off."

In issuing these orders, Colonel de Haldimar evinced a composedness that astonished all who heard him. But although his voice was calm, despair was upon his brow. Still he continued to gaze fixedly on the retreating form of his enemy, until he finally disappeared behind the orchard of the Canadian of the Fleur de lis.

Obeying the summons from the fort, the troops without now commenced their retreat, bearing off the bodies of their fallen officers and several of their comrades who had fallen by the Indian fire. There was a show of harassing them on their return; but they were too near the fort to apprehend much danger. Two or three well-directed discharges of artillery effectually checked the onward progress of the savages; and, in the course of a minute, they had again wholly disappeared.

In gloomy silence, and with anger and disappointment in their hearts, the detachment now re-entered the fort. Johnstone was only severely bruised; Sir Everard Valletort not dead. Both were conveyed to the same room, where they were instantly attended by the surgeon, who pronounced the situation of the latter hopeless.

Major Blackwater, Captains Blessington and Erskine, Lieutenants Leslie and Boyce, and Ensigns Fortescue and Summers, were now the only regimental officers that remained of thirteen originally comprising the strength of the garrison. The whole of these stood grouped around their colonel, who seemed transfixed to the spot he had first occupied on the rampart, with his arms folded, and his gaze bent in the direction in which he had lost sight of Wacousta and his child.

Hitherto the morning had been cold and cheerless, and objects in the far distance were but indistinctly seen through a humid atmosphere. At about half an hour before mid-day the air became more rarified, and, the murky clouds gradually disappearing, left the blue autumnal sky without spot or blemish. Presently, as the bells of the fort struck twelve, a yell as of a legion of devils rent the air; and, riveting their gaze in that direction, all beheld the bridge, hitherto deserted, suddenly covered with a multitude of savages, among whom were several individuals attired in the European garb, and evidently prisoners. Each officer had a telescope raised to his eye, and each prepared himself, shudderingly, for some horrid consummation. Presently the bridge was cleared of all but a double line of what appeared to be women, armed with war-clubs and tomahawks. Along the line were now seen to pass, in slow succession, the prisoners that had previously been observed. At each step they took (and it was evident they had been compelled to run the gauntlet), a blow was inflicted by some one or other of the line, until the wretched victims were successively despatched. A loud yell from the warriors, who, although hidden from view by the intervening orchards, were evidently merely spectators in the bloody drama, announced each death. These yells were repeated, at intervals, to about the number of thirty, when, suddenly, the bridge was again deserted as before.

After the lapse of a minute, the tall figure of a warrior was seen to advance, holding a female in his arms. No one could mistake, even at that distance, the gigantic proportions of Wacousta,—as he stood in the extreme centre of the bridge, in imposing relief against the flood that glittered like a sea of glass beyond. From his chest there now burst a single yell; but, although audible, it was fainter than any remembered ever to have been heard from him by the garrison. He then advanced to the extreme edge of the bridge; and, raising the form of the female far above his head with his left hand, seemed to wave her in vengeful triumph. A second warrior was seen upon the bridge, and stealing cautiously to the same point. The right hand of the first warrior was now raised and brandished in air; in the next instant it descended upon the breast of the female, who fell from his arms into the ravine beneath. Yells of triumph from the Indians, and shouts of execration from the soldiers, mingled faintly together. At that moment the arm of the second warrior was raised, and a blade was seen to glitter in the sunshine. His arm descended, and Wacousta was observed to stagger forward and fall heavily into the abyss into which his victim had the instant before been precipitated. Another loud yell, but of disappointment and anger, was heard drowning that of exultation pealed by the triumphant warrior, who, darting to the open extremity of the bridge, directed his flight along the margin of the river, where a light canoe was ready to receive him. Into this he sprang, and, seizing the paddle, sent the waters foaming from its sides; and, pursuing his way across the river, had nearly gained the shores of Canada before a bark was to be seen following in pursuit.

How felt—how acted Colonel de Haldimar throughout this brief but terrible scene? He uttered not a word. With his arms still folded across his breast, he gazed upon the murder of his child; but he heaved not a groan, he shed not a tear. A momentary triumph seemed to, irradiate his pallid features, when he saw the blow struck that annihilated his enemy; but it was again instantly shaded by an expression of the most profound despair.

"It is done, gentlemen," he at length remarked. "The tragedy is closed, the curse of Ellen Halloway is fulfilled, and I am—childless!—Blackwater," he pursued, endeavouring to stifle the emotion produced by the last reflection, "pay every attention to the security of the garrison, see that the drawbridge is again properly chained up, and direct that the duties of the troops be prosecuted in every way as heretofore."

Leaving his officers to wonder at and pity that apathy of mind that could mingle the mere forms of duty with the most heart-rending associations, Colonel de Haldimar now quitted the rampart; and, with a head that was remarked for the first time to droop over his chest, paced his way musingly to his apartments.

CHAPTER XIV.

Night had long since drawn her circling mantle over the western hemisphere; and deeper, far deeper than the gloom of that night was the despair which filled every bosom of the devoted garrison, whose fortunes it has fallen to our lot to record. A silence, profound as that of death, pervaded the ramparts and exterior defences of the fortress, interrupted only, at long intervals, by the customary "All's well!" of the several sentinels; which, after the awful events of the day, seemed to many who now heard it as if uttered in mockery of their hopelessness of sorrow. The lights within the barracks of the men had been long since extinguished; and, consigned to a mere repose of limb, in which the eye and heart shared not, the inferior soldiery pressed their rude couches with spirits worn out by a succession of painful excitements, and frames debilitated, by much abstinence and watching. It was an hour at which sleep was wont to afford them the blessing of a temporary forgetfulness of endurances that weighed the more heavily as they were believed to be endless and without fruit; but sleep had now apparently been banished from all; for the low and confused murmur that met the ear from the several block-houses was continuous and general, betraying at times, and in a louder key, words that bore reference to the tragic occurrences of the day.

The only lights visible in the fort proceeded from the guard-house and a room adjoining that of the ill-fated Charles de Haldimar. Within the latter were collected, with the exception of the governor, and grouped around a bed on which lay one of their companions in a nearly expiring state, the officers of the garrison, reduced nearly one third in number since we first offered them to the notice of our readers. The dying man was Sir Everard Valletort, who, supported by pillows, was concluding a narrative that had chained the earnest attention of his auditory, even amid the deep and heartfelt sympathy perceptible in each for the forlorn and hopeless condition of the narrator. At the side of the unhappy baronet, and enveloped in a dressing gown, as if recently out of bed, sat, reclining in a rude elbow chair, one whose pallid countenance denoted, that, although far less seriously injured, he, too, had suffered severely:—it was Lieutenant Johnstone.

The narrative was at length closed; and the officer, exhausted by the effort he had made in his anxiety to communicate every particular to his attentive and surprised companions, had sunk back upon his pillow, when, suddenly, the loud and unusual "Who comes there?" of the sentinel stationed on the rampart above the gateway, arrested every ear. A moment of pause succeeded, when again was heard the "Stand, friend!" evidently given in reply to the familiar answer to the original challenge. Then were audible rapid movements in the guard-house, as of men aroused from temporary slumber, and hastening to the point whence the voice proceeded.

Silently yet hurriedly the officers now quitted the bedside of the dying man, leaving only the surgeon and the invalid Johnstone behind them; and, flying to the rampart, stood in the next minute confounded with the guard, who were already grouped round the challenging sentinel, bending their gaze eagerly in the direction of the road.

"What now, man?—whom have you challenged?" asked Major Blackwater.

"It is I—De Haldimar," hoarsely exclaimed one of four dark figures that, hitherto, unnoticed by the officers, stood immediately beyond the ditch, with a burden deposited at their feet. "Quick, Blackwater, let us in for God's sake! Each succeeding minute may bring a scouting party on our track. Lower the drawbridge!"

"Impossible!" exclaimed the major: "after all that has passed, it is more than my commission is worth to lower the bridge without permission. Mr. Lawson, quick to the governor, and report that Captain de Haldimar is here: with whom shall he say?" again addressing the impatient and almost indignant officer.

"With Miss de Haldimar, Francois the Canadian, and one to whom we all owe our lives," hurriedly returned the officer; "and you may add," he continued gloomily, "the corpse of my sister. But while we stand in parley here, we are lost: Lawson, fly to my father, and tell him we wait for entrance."

With nearly the speed enjoined the adjutant departed. Scarcely a minute elapsed when he again stood upon the rampart, and advancing closely to the major, whispered a few words in his ear.

"Good God! can it be possible? When? How came this? but we will enquire later. Open the gate; down with the bridge, Leslie," addressing the officer of the guard.

The command was instantly obeyed. The officers flew to receive the fugitives; and as the latter crossed the drawbridge, the light of a lantern, that had been brought from the guard-room, flashed full upon the harassed countenances of Captain and Miss de Haldimar, Francois the Canadian, and the devoted Oucanasta.

Silent and melancholy was the greeting that took place between the parties: the voice spoke not; the hand alone was eloquent; but it was in the eloquence of sorrow only that it indulged. Pleasure, even in this almost despaired of re-union, could not be expressed; and even the eye shrank from mutual encounter, as if its very glance at such a moment were sacrilege. Recalled to a sense of her situation by the preparation of the men to raise the bridge, the Indian woman was the first to break the silence.

"The Saganaw is safe within his fort, and the girl of the pale faces will lay her head upon his bosom," she remarked solemnly. "Oucanasta will go to her solitary wigwam among the red skins."

The heart of Madeline de Haldimar was oppressed by the weight of many griefs; yet she could not see the generous preserver of her life, and the rescuer of the body of her ill-fated cousin, depart without emotion. Drawing a ring, of some value and great beauty, from her finger, which she had more than once observed the Indian to admire, she placed it on her hand; and then, throwing herself on the bosom of the faithful creature, embraced her with deep manifestations of affection, but without uttering a word.

Oucanasta was sensibly gratified: she raised her large eyes to heaven as if in thankfulness; and by the light of the lantern, which fell upon her dark but expressive countenance, tears were to be seen starting unbidden from their source.

Released from the embrace of her, whose life she had twice preserved at imminent peril to her own, the Indian again prepared to depart; but there was another, who, like Madeline, although stricken by many sorrows, could not forego the testimony of his heart's gratitude. Captain de Haldimar, who, during this short scene, had despatched a messenger to his room for the purpose, now advanced to the poor girl, bearing a short but elegantly mounted dagger, which he begged her to deliver as a token of his friendship to the young chief her brother. He then dropped on one knee at her feet, and raising her hand, pressed it fervently against his heart; an action which, even to the untutored mind of the Indian, bore evidence only of the feeling that prompted it, A heavy sigh escaped her labouring chest; and as the officer now rose and quitted her hand, she turned slowly and with dignity from him, and crossing the drawbridge, was in a few minutes lost in the surrounding gloom.

Our readers have, doubtless, anticipated the communication made to Major Blackwater by the Adjutant Lawson. Bowed down to the dust by the accomplishment of the curse of Ellen Halloway, the inflexibility of Colonel de Haldimar's pride was not proof against the utter annihilation wrought to his hopes as a father by the unrelenting hatred of the enemy his early falsehood and treachery had raised up to him. When the adjutant entered his apartment, the stony coldness of his cheek attested he had been dead some hours.

We pass over the few days of bitter trial that succeeded to the restoration of Captain de Haldimar and his bride to their friends; days, during which were consigned to the same grave the bodies of the governor, his lamented children, and the scarcely less regretted Sir Everard Valletort. The funeral service was attempted by Captain Blessington; but the strong affection of that excellent officer, for three of the defunct parties at least, was not armed against the trial. He had undertaken a task far beyond his strength; and scarcely had commenced, ere he was compelled to relinquish the performance of the ritual to the adjutant. A large grave had been dug close under the rampart, and near the fatal flag-staff, to receive the bodies of their deceased friends; and, as they were lowered successively into their last earthly resting place, tears fell unrestrainedly over the bronzed cheeks of the oldest soldiers, while many a female sob blended with and gave touching solemnity to the scene.

On the morning of the third day from this quadruple interment, notice was given by one of the sentinels that an Indian was approaching the fort, making signs as if in demand for a parley. The officers, headed by Major Blackwater, now become the commandant of the place, immediately ascended the rampart, when the stranger was at once recognised by Captain de Haldimar for the young Ottawa, the preserver of his life, and the avenger of the deaths of those they mourned, in whose girdle was thrust, in seeming pride, the richly mounted dagger that officer had caused to be conveyed to him through his no less generous sister. A long conference ensued, in the language of the Ottawas, between the parties just named, the purport of which was of high moment to the garrison, now nearly reduced to the last extremity. The young chief had come to apprise them, that, won by the noble conduct of the English, on a late occasion, when his warriors were wholly in their power, Ponteac had expressed a generous determination to conclude a peace with the garrison, and henceforth to consider them as his friends. This he had publicly declared in a large council of the chiefs, held the preceding night; and the motive of the Ottawa's coming was, to assure the English, that, on this occasion, their great leader was perfectly sincere in a resolution, at which he had the more readily arrived, now that his terrible coadjutor and vindictive adviser was no more. He prepared them for the coming of Ponteac and the principal chiefs of the league to demand a

266

council on the morrow; and, with this final communication, again withdrew.

The Ottawa was right Within a week from that period the English were to be seen once more issuing from their fort; and, although many months elapsed before the wounds of their suffering hearts were healed, still were they grateful to Providence for their final preservation from a doom that had fallen, without exception, on every fortress on the line of frontier in which they lay.

Time rolled on; and, in the course of years, Oucanasta might be seen associating with and bearing curious presents, the fruits of Indian ingenuity, to the daughters of De Haldimar, now become the colonel of the —— regiment; while her brother, the chief, instructed his sons in the athletic and active exercises peculiar to his race. As for poor Ellen Halloway, search had been made for her, but she never was heard of afterwards.

THE END

CONTENTS

CPSIA information can be obtained
at www.ICGtesting.com
Printed in the USA
LVHW102235150223
739387LV00028B/612